Mills & Boon Classics

A chance to read and collect some of the best-loved novels from Mills & Boon – the world's largest publisher of romantic fiction.

Every month, four titles by favourite Mills & Boon authors will be re-published in the *Classics* series.

A list of other titles in the *Classics* series can be found at the end of this book.

Mary Wibberley

BLACK NIALL

MILLS & BOON LIMITED
LONDON · TORONTO

First published 1973
Australian copyright 1980
Philippine copyright 1980
This edition 1980

© Mary Wibberley 1973

ISBN 0 263 73378 5

Set in 11/12½ pt. Linotype Baskerville

*Made and printed in Great Britain by
Richard Clay (The Chaucer Press) Ltd,
Bungay, Suffolk*

CHAPTER ONE

Nobody knew that Niall MacBain was coming home to Shielbaig until the stormy summer day he arrived.

Alison Mackay was sitting in the classroom, when her attention wandered from the laborious account of Robert the Bruce that Willy MacLeod was giving to his six fellow pupils. From the height of her desk, she saw a flash of blue through the trees and rain, and something made her go to the window.

'Carry on reading, Willy,' she told the boy, as he faltered. 'We're all listening.' She waited for the car to reappear. It was difficult to see anything, for the driving rain gave the village below the school a misty appearance. And what would anyone be wanting there midweek in late June? They were off the beaten tourist track, completely isolated save for the mobile shops twice a week, and even they would be parked somewhere safe in this. Thunder rumbled distantly, threatening, like a growling dog half asleep.

Then she saw the car again, as it came half-way up the village's only street, and stopped almost on the shingle of Loch Shiel, now grey and leaden in the strange half light of a storm. Alison shivered, some premonition of trouble making her cold, although the small classroom was warm with the peat fire that glowed in the corner. She watched the faint blurred figure of a man get out and run across the street, then vanish into one of the cottages. She wasn't sure, but it seemed as if it was the one belonging to old Fergus

MacBain.

A waiting silence made her turn. 'Fine, Willy, that was fine,' she looked at her watch. A quarter to four, and there would be no more work done today, for the storm was making the children restless, and one or two seemed frightened. Alison crossed to the desk. 'Get your coats, children. I'll take you all home.' She smiled at the ensuing hubbub, thankful that she'd come in the car that morning, for even though she lived barely a mile away, she would have been drenched after walking only a few yards.

Checking that the fireguard was secured, Alison switched out the light, plunging the place into premature gloom, and stood them all in the porch while she dashed round the back for her car.

One by one she deposited the giggling children at their doors, as they drove down the hilly street. One, Fiona Stewart, lived next door to old Fergus MacBain, and Alison said casually, as she leaned back to open the door for her: 'My, it looks as if Mr. MacBain has a visitor.' She felt rather than saw the odd look the girl gave her. Fiona was very mature for a ten-year-old, and everybody knew about the feud; it had passed into village folklore. But all she said was:

'Aye, miss.'

There was a light in the cottage. Alison pretended she was watching Fiona as she stood in the porch, but it was the glow of the oil lamp from the front window that really fascinated her. And even then, some presentiment of who it could be was hovering, tantalizingly, at the back of her brain.

Alison had so many other things on her mind that she

had forgotten the incident when she reached home. Jessie heard her putting the car outside the back door to garage later when the storm was over, and she opened it wide.

'Come away in, child,' she called, her white hair in a fuzzy halo round her from the light behind. Alison ran thankfully in and smiled.

'What a day, Jessie! Is there tea in the pot?'

'I have the kettle on now. Sit ye down. I want a word before you go in.'

'I'll make it,' Alison protested, as Jessie waved her away, and sniffed.

'No, you won't. There is only one person knows how to make tea in this house, and that's me.'

Alison grinned at her from the rocking chair as she coasted gently backwards and forwards. 'Yes, Jessie, sorry, Jessie. I don't know what we'd do without you.' And in her words was more than jest. She meant them, quite seriously. She watched the old woman, her bony hands confident and capable as she lifted the heavy kettle from where it bubbled on the range. She had been with the family since before Alison was born; even before her brother Alec who was five years older. And now, with their father dead, and Alec married in Canada, and their money vanished like a will o'-the-wisp, Jessie was still with them, firm and immovable.

A tower of strength, she had kept Alison's mother going in those difficult days three years before when Mr. Mackay's plane had crashed over the sea as he was on his way to Jugoslavia for a business conference. He had been on the verge of a breakthrough in his engineering firm in Inverness, one that would mean new wealth and security, sadly depleted owing to a trusted partner's dishonesty.

What little they had had been swallowed up in death duties after the tragic blow. But Jessie had remained, and, Alison hoped, would for as long as she lived. She loved the old housekeeper dearly.

Jessie put the teapot firmly on its stand, then looked over at Alison. 'It's your mother. She's acting strange again, wandering around and getting in my way, instead of on with her painting. And she's got that dreamy look on her face – the one she gets when she's got an idea fixed firmly in her mind. I don't know what it can be, but I've got an awful good idea.'

Alison nodded, her heart plunging down to her shoes.

'The house?'

'Aye.' She watched Alison shrewdly, her blue eyes bright and youthful in her wrinkled, beautiful old face. 'She's been going on for the past few months about it being too big, and too dear to run, and all sorts of things—'

'I know,' Alison interrupted miserably. 'But she always does in summer, when the sun shows up all the faults. I – oh, Jessie, what can we do?'

Jessie looked around the huge high-ceilinged kitchen. 'God knows, child. She's right. What can three women do in a house this size? There's your money, and the bit Alec sends, and what your mother makes from her paintings – such as *that* is, but we all know it's not enough—'

'She can't sell the house. It's been in the family for generations,' Alison said desperately. 'And anyway,' as a thought came to her, 'who'd buy it? We all know these big houses are a glut on the market. Oh, Jessie!'

8

She put her hands over her eyes for a moment. 'I hope we're wrong.'

'Aye, but we ought to find out. You had better ask her – and be kind, Alison. You know how she gets upset at any unpleasantness.'

Alison managed a smile. 'I should do by now. Thanks for telling me, Jessie. Perhaps we can work something out, who knows?' She said it lightly, but her heart was as heavy as lead. She loved her home with a fierce pride. It was a large beautiful granite building facing the loch, capturing all the sun, shielding them from the wildest storms and rains, and surrounded by trees and mountains in the loveliest part of Scotland, Wester Ross. And now, as she walked from the kitchen to the hall, a flash of lightning illumined the gloom for a second, and she shivered.

It was much later that evening before she learned the truth that ended all her speculations.

Alison was curled up on the settee in the lounge, marking exercise books, and looked across at her mother, to surprise an odd, almost furtive look on her face as she looked back from the book that lay on her knee. She was normally so open, almost transparent, that Alison could bear it no longer. She put down the book beside her.

'Mother,' she said gently, 'tell me – please.'

Mrs. Mackay blinked, opened her eyes wide, and looked, if anything more guilty than ever. Alison felt a surge of love for her, a lump in her throat that she quickly swallowed. Her mother was so fragile and helpless-looking that she had to make a conscious effort to remember that this slender dark-haired woman had, in her younger days, been a successful interior designer and decorator, had travelled the world under her own steam, with another girl, before being swept off her feet by Alison's father, on a holiday in Australia. She had come home, married him, and settled down to being a laird's wife. And no one had ever heard her utter a word of regret for the undoubted fame and fortune that could have been hers if she had gone on with her career. Now she confined herself to oil paintings of the Highlands, and occasionally sold some to Murdoch Imrie, an old friend of the family who owned a madly expensive antique shop in Inverness.

'Tell you what?' But her hand went to her cheek in a curiously fluttering gesture, a sure giveaway with her.

Alison went over and sat at her feet, resting her head on her mother's knee. 'Oh, Mother! Both Jessie and I are concerned for you. There's something on your mind. You're going to have to tell me sooner or later. Why not now?' The logic of this was inescapable. She sighed, and stroked Alison's hair gently.

'All right, I know. Oh, Alison, it's something – I should have told you before, because I don't like to be underhand – and you should know, above all—' her voice broke, then as if gathering her courage together, she went on: 'Things have reached the stage where it's impossible to go on much longer. We'll have to sell the house.'

Alison looked at her, blinking back tears at having the fears finally confirmed. 'That's what we thought. But I love it so.'

'So do I,' her mother answered softly. 'Oh, I've given it a lot of thought, and perhaps I should have discussed it with you sooner, but – well, I kept hoping – you know how I do.' Alison nodded, unhappy for her mother as much as for herself.

'I've already had a word with Mr. Stewart—' Alison looked up sharply. John Stewart had been the family solicitor for years; he was almost like an uncle. It was the sensible thing to do, she knew, yet it made it so definite.

'What did he say?'

Her mother gave a faint smile. 'You won't believe this, but there's someone interested in Courthill. He wouldn't tell me who it was, but apparently a person – I don't even know if it's a man or woman – contacted him a year or so ago, and asked to be informed if ever Courthill came on to the market. It must be someone who's seen it. He phoned me yesterday. This person will be contacting us soon.' She looked to the fireplace, where the peat fire glowed dully, nearly out. 'That's why I've been on edge these past few days,' she squeezed Alison's shoulder. 'Forgive me. I have no choice.'

'No.' Alison shook her head. 'Surely there's something?'

'What? I wish there were. You know what it's like here in winter, when we virtually hibernate because the house is like an ice-box. We should have had central heating installed years ago. It was all right when we were filled with visitors, fires in every room, and people, and warmth, but not any more. There are only the three of us, and Jessie is old. How long do you think she can go on working in that huge draughty kitchen? She never grumbles, she's an angel, but it will tell on her soon.'

The storm had died away. It reflected Alison's mood now, quieter, and suddenly resigned. She sighed, and turned her head to where Rusty, their golden labrador, lay stretched out fast asleep on the hearthrug. She was old, a little grey now, and Alison reached out a hand to stroke her. The dog stirred slightly in her sleep. 'Mother, where will we go?'

'I've been looking at the cottage in the grounds. It's so long since we had a gardener that it needs a lot doing up, but it could be done. And it's big enough for the three of us, and Rusty.'

'And Rusty,' Alison echoed. 'But can you do that? Sell the house and not the cottage?'

'Of course.' Her mother looked surprised. 'It's virtually separate anyway. We'll keep the small garden round it, and we have the same view of the loch as we have from here.'

All she said was true. But would she be able to bear it, living so close, with someone else in her house? Alison wondered silently. That was the question, and there was no way to answer it, except one.

They went to bed, and Alison still hadn't told her mother about the other thing that was bothering her. It was just as well. Mrs. Mackay had enough on her plate, but Alison's burden was doubled. It was almost certain that the school would have to close after the autumn term. Of the seven children she taught, five would be leaving at Christmas because they were almost eleven, and would be going as weekly boarders to Dingwall. The other two would then be transferred to the school in Strathcorran, which was fifteen miles away. And as there were no children above the age of one in Shielbaig, the school would remain closed for four years – if

where it fell steeply away into the sea, and he had seen the two men locked in fierce combat. The ground was treacherous and covered in loose stones and pebbles, and even as he had watched, they had slipped and gone hurtling over the edge, still fighting.

By the time he had managed to reach the spot, it was too late. Far below, the white foamy sea crashed against the rocks, and the noise of the breakers, and the harsh cry of the gulls, were the only sounds left in the world. Sick with shock, he had turned away.

When his tale was told, bitter, unforgivable words had been spoken. And from that day on, the two families had become as far apart as the two poles, hatred sparking like a live current if any should meet. There was more too, but the tales were only vaguely hinted at; tales of smuggling, and gambling, and illicit whisky stills.

But no one had ever told Alison exactly what. Perhaps there was shame of a different kind on both sides, she thought. Certainly she knew that she had never dared ask when she was a child, and now it was too late. Sometimes she wondered if Alec had ever found out.

Alison lived at Courthill, the family home since long before the feud, and Fergus MacBain, the last remaining member of his family in the area, lived in a small cottage that had been his father's and grandfather's before him. The big house that had once been theirs, so near to Courthill, had been destroyed by a terrible fire in 1872, and all their money, so the story ran, had gone with it. In its place grew trees, and all that remained to tell that there had once been a house were a few heaps of stone.

Alison shivered, suddenly cold at the memories revived, and joined in with the children's exercises with
such enthusiasm, as if to shake away the ghosts of the
past, that they were startled, and couldn't keep up with
her pace. Her mind refused to join in with the later
lessons. She was weighed down with an intense feeling
of depression. It was probably the knowledge that the
school might have to close, or it could have been caused
by the thought of leaving her home – or a combination
of the two. It brought on a headache that persisted
even after she had taken two aspirins, and by four
o'clock she was so wretched that it was a relief to see the
children go. She sat very still at her desk and watched
them run shrieking and shouting down the hill, as if
released from prison.

Distantly, on the other side of the loch, she could see
home. Just the roof, and part of a bedroom window
over the thick trees, but it was enough to bring a lump
to her throat. How can I leave it? she thought. Tears of
pain and fatigue sprang to her eyes. She was being
childish, she knew. Her mother was right. They could
not go on living there, managing as they did, and
expect the house to maintain itself. She wasn't so
blinded by love for it that she couldn't see the window
frames that needed attention, or the slates missing from
the roof. Even the grounds had deteriorated rapidly
since they had let the gardener go. Alison and her
mother did their best, but it was fighting a losing battle
with the acres of rich vegetation that ran riot, sheltered
as they were in the curve of the bay of the loch.

She sighed, picked up her mirror, and dabbed carefully at her eyes. There must be no trace of tears when
she reached home. She looked at herself coldly and

critically, seeing only the slight damp smudges on her cheeks. She was not aware of what others could see, the rare inner beauty that shone through, lighting her features so that everyone she met was immediately drawn to her. Her mouth was full and feminine, softly curved; her eyes an attractive shade of deep blue, fringed by long lashes, with finely shaped brows slanting serenely above them. Both brows and lashes were thick and dark.

She put the mirror away, flicked a comb through rebelliously curly hair, then went round, checking that all was safely in its place. The school was quiet without the children, silent and lifeless.

Alison's headache went as she began the walk down into the village a few minutes later. She had to call at the post office for some airmail forms for Jessie, who carried on a prolific correspondence with nieces and nephews in all parts of the world. It was pleasant, greeting the friendly-faced villagers as she went along, feeling at home there as she knew she would nowhere else.

The post office, which also served as grocery, greengrocery, newsagent and ironmongers, was at the end of the village round a bend in the road on Alison's way home, and invisible from the school. As she reached it, she half turned to wave to Mr. MacIntyre, sitting repairing his nets on the beach, and, turning back, cannoned right into a man who was coming out of the post office at the same moment. For a split second she was winded with the impact; felt two strong arms steadying her, then looked up. And in that startled instant of mutual recognition she gasped and pulled herself away as if from the fatal embrace of a snake. The man she had cannoned into so violently, and who was looking at her with the strangest expression, was none other than Niall MacBain. Black Niall himself! Recovering, Alison moved to one side and hurried into the dark, paraffin-smelling shop, her heart beating violently. She was horribly aware that he still stood outside, looking through the dark window.

'A dozen airmails, please, Mrs. Finlayson,' she said. Her arms still burned from his touch, where he had steadied her, and her skin crawled at the memory. Of all the sons – that it should be *him*, the one she loathed most, who had come back home to his father's house!

Mrs. Finlayson regarded Alison with bright beady eyes, her head slightly tilted to one side in excitement.

'There now, Miss Mackay. Did you not see who was just in here? Fergus MacBain's youngest, Niall!'

'I saw him, yes,' Alison answered.

Mrs. Finlayson clicked her teeth. 'Ach now, I was forgetting! It is so long since the boys were home, and your brother away to Canada, that it seems as if the feud has been forgotten.' She chuckled, the malicious gleam in her bright eyes belying her next words. 'But there, now. It is nothing to do with me at all, is it?'

'Oh, that!' And Alison laughed, determined not to let the other woman see that anything was amiss. 'That was long ago.'

'Aye, no doubt.' As Alison paid for the blue airmail forms, Mrs. Finlayson said: 'Ach, I must away and send this telegram. Eh, Rio is in South America, is it not?'

'Rio? Yes, Brazil.' Alison took her change, smiled her thanks, and escaped. There was no sign of Niall Mac-

Bain when she got out into the fresh air, and she took a deep breath. It was bad enough to see him, but to have bumped into him as well! She rubbed her arm, as if to erase his touch, and walked quickly homewards, trying desperately to push to the back of her mind the awful, humiliating memory of that last time she had met him, nine years before. It was no use. As she walked down the familiar road, thickly wooded on either side, and with no sound save her own footsteps, the picture she had tried so hard to forget came bustling forward as if anxious for release.

It had been so near there too. Alison was almost sixteen at the time, and Alec twenty-one. There had been a dance in Shielbaig on the Saturday night, and their parents had let her go, provided that she came home with him. There had been a big crowd in the wooden Institute Hall, and the night had been hot, noisy, and tremendously exciting. For Alison had discovered, to her delighted surprise, that she was much in demand for all the dances, and had spent the entire evening being swept – almost literally – off her feet on the soapflake-covered floor, in various male arms. An added fillip was the glimpse she had, early in the evening, of Niall MacBain standing by the door, in the crowd, just watching, as if shy and unsure of himself. He wore an ill-fitting blue suit, shiny at the elbows, and looked desperately ill at ease. Alison knew he was watching her, and it made her all the more determined to let the world see what a wonderful time she was having. Some instinct of female coquetry, one she barely understood, must have been at work, for each time she whirled past and looked, ever so casually, his eyes were on her. She laughed, eyes sparkling, into her partner's faces, and more than one tried to steal a kiss in that dismal corrugated iron-roofed shed that had become paradise for one magical evening.

But, like Cinderella's Ball, the evening had to end, and when it did, and Alison tried to find Alec, he was nowhere to be seen. As people drifted away, she looked around, wishing she had kept a closer eye on him. But she had been having too good a time to bother, and now . . . 'See you home, Alison?' A voice came from the darkness, and she whirled round to see one of her more enthusiastic partners, a handsome boy named Johnny Gordon, from Strathcorran, watching her.

'N-no, thanks.' She was suddenly uneasy. It was one thing to flirt with gay abandon at a dance – quite another to be walking home with a young man who had a reputation as a wolf. 'I'm meeting Alec down the road,' she lied, and with a careless wave, ran off into the darkness. Where, oh, where was he?

Once away from the hall she slowed down. She wasn't nervous of the dark, and enjoyed walking. She was busy planning a few things to say to her brother, when she sensed she was being followed, and began to walk a little quicker. She was near a short cut, leading directly into the grounds of Courthill, and scrambled over the low stone wall, breaking a nail in her haste. Then she was in the thick sweet-smelling pines. Branches caught spitefully at her hair as she half ran, half walked through the moonlit gloom. Then something made her turn and stop, as she heard unmistakably, from somewhere close behind, the sound of fighting. There were grunts, then cracks, as if of fist meeting face, the obvious sound of crashing in the undergrowth as someone went sprawling, then voices, low and urgent. Running footsteps faded into the distance. Alec? Could it be Alec who had seen someone following her, and caught up with him? Alison wondered. She waited, but there was no further sound.

'Alec?' She said it quietly at first, then louder as there was no reply. Quickly she retraced her steps, came into the clearing by the trout stream, and stopped dead in utter astonishment as she saw her arch-enemy, Niall MacBain, standing with his back partially to her, rubbing his knuckles. Immediately, knowing how he and Alec spent their lives battling, she dashed forward.

'What have you done with my brother?' she demanded, so angry that she caught his arm.

He turned round slowly, and she remembered thinking, as he did, how different he was. He had been like a fish out of water in the crowded hall. Now he seemed to have grown, and was no longer ill at ease. He looked down at her, and even in the misty cold light of the half hidden moon, Alison saw the contempt on his face as he said:

'I've done nothing wi' your brother.' He shook his arm free. 'The one who's just now run away like a rabbit was Johnny Gordon. He was following you.'

'I don't believe you!' But she saw the blood on his chin, welling from a cut under his mouth, even as she said the words.

He shrugged. 'Do you think *I* care whether you believe me or not?' His mouth twisted. 'The way you were behaving tonight, it's a wonder you didn't have a few more after you!'

'What do you mean by that?' she demanded, glad

that he could not see the hot colour rushing to her cheeks.

'You're nearly sixteen, you should know,' was the brutal answer.

Alison drew breath in sharply. 'How *dare* you speak to me like that! If Alec was here, he'd soon—'

'Aye, but he's not, is he? And do you think I'm frightened of him?' He gave a mocking laugh. 'You should see what I just did to Johnny.'

'That's all you think about, fighting, isn't it?' she ground out furiously, and at the same time angry with herself. 'You're always fighting.'

'I wouldn't say that – not all the time.' He grinned suddenly, and reached out to touch Alison's face. Startled, she hit his arm away, and backed a few inches. 'Don't touch me!' she said. 'Don't ever do that again!'

'You didn't mind everyone else doing it at the dance,' he retorted. 'In fact, I'd say you looked as if you were enjoying every minute of it.' He suddenly pulled her towards him, catching her off balance, and so much by surprise that she was in his arms before she knew what was happening.

'Let's see what everyone found so wonderful.' And he kissed her hard on the lips, taking her breath away. Then as abruptly he released her, and stood before her, his chest heaving.

Sobbing with the shock of it all, and deeply disturbed at her own reaction, Alison slapped him hard across his face. Before she could turn to run, his hand shot out and held her arm. She gasped with fear, suddenly remembering his fiery hot temper, and tried to pull away, frightened. Then he laughed. 'You're safe enough,' he might have read her mind. 'I never hit *girls*. But I don't like being slapped by them either.'

'Let me go!' She suddenly realized something else. 'You – you were following me as well.' Her teeth began chattering as she realized the implications, and she twisted desperately, trying to free herself from a grip of steel.

'Aye, but I was coming this way anyway.' He released her abruptly. 'I fancied taking home a few trout for supper – so—' and he looked first at the stream, then at Alison, as if challenging her to say anything. She couldn't meet his glance, and looked away. Shame mingled with the impotent rage she felt at his bold, rough manner. They had seldom spoken before. The feud was like a shadow between them, one that coloured Alec's and her lives, and she hated him for forcing her gratitude, hated him also for that rough male kiss, taken so abruptly and cruelly. It had been her first kiss . . . She had not imagined it would be like that – or from him.

'That would be poaching,' she said eventually, trying to sound firm and authoritative.

'Poaching?' He threw back his head and laughed. 'Poaching, eh? Well, *Miss* Mackay, it won't be the first time I've poached here – or the last.'

'You – what do you mean?' Astonishment had replaced fear. A deep instinct told Alison that he would not harm her, though she did not know why.

'What do you mean?' he mimicked cruelly. 'Are you daft? What do you think I mean? I've been here hundreds of times. Aye, and my brothers too. And your precious gardener, and Alec, even your dogs – they've never known.'

'I'll tell them,' she said. 'I'll have you arrested!'

'Och, you'll have me trembling in my boots! Try it, and you'll all be the laughing stock of Shielbaig. Where's your proof?'

'I'll tell them what you said.'

'Will you now?' He cocked his head to one side. 'And have them ask me how I got this cut on my chin?' He dabbed at the dark patch with a handkerchief. 'What will you have me tell them, eh? That *you* were fighting me? Or the truth?' A smile broadened his mouth, and Alison clenched her fists, hating him more than ever. He was loathsome! He had an answer for everything, and she was only wasting time talking to him; worse, being made to look foolish. She stood up straight and glared coldly at him.

'Take your trout,' she said clearly, 'and go. You must feel entitled to some payment for your so *gallant* rescue. The trout will do.' She knew that her words had stung him, by the quick darkening of his face, as he spat out: 'It's a pity someone can't take you down a peg or two, Miss High-and-Mighty.'

'Who – you? Don't make me laugh!' She turned and began to walk away. His voice came after her.

'Aye, maybe – one day.'

Alison ran home then, and never told anyone what had happened, not even Alec, who had been flirting round the back of the hall with a girl, and who got a telling off from their mother for not seeing her safely home.

She had passed the trout stream now, and she bit her lip at the memory of those last bitter words of Niall MacBain's. They had obviously been said in a fit of temper, for shortly afterwards, only months in fact, he had left home, and she had not seen him since.

The contrast between the thin, long-legged, gangly youth wtih his fiery temper and the man she had bumped into was enormous. He had filled out, his shoulders broad and powerful. The dark, intense boy was now mature. His deeply tanned face was a mocking reminder of the youngster she had so hated, older, the lines of experience lending an interest to what, before, had been the promise of good looks. All this, Alison had seen in that split second of mutual recognition. The eyes – she would never forget his eyes, as he had looked at her. They were changed; older, wiser, more cynical. Deep grey, the colour of the loch in winter, there had been a disturbing expression that had worried her, and made her pull herself away so quickly.

She walked on homeward, lost in thought, knowing that Jessie at least would be interested when Alison told her who she had seen. The feud had always fascinated her. Not so Alison's mother, who had always been distressed at Alec's eagerness to fight with the youngest MacBain and couldn't see why something that had happened so long ago should affect their lives like it did.

But when Alison went into the house, she forgot everything at the sight of her mother's face. She came running down the stairs as Alison pushed open the heavy front door. There was an air of suppressed excitement about her as she greeted her daughter, and Alison said: 'Mother? What is it?'

'I've just now had a call from John Stewart. The man who is interested in buying our house – he's coming to see it tomorrow!'

Alison's heart gave an unpleasant lurch, and she looked at her mother in dismay. There was something else about her mother too, something puzzling. 'Oh, I see,' she said.

'And Alison—'

'Yes?'

'Oh – er – nothing.' But her hand went to her face, and Alison sensed sudden distress.

'Mother? What is it? Have you had second thoughts—'

'No, no – it's – I don't feel very well.' And she ran up the stairs as if someone were after her. Alison stood there watching, and thought her mother had had an attack of nerves. She didn't know what had caused her distress. She was to wish later that she had asked.

She woke with leaden heart next morning, and bathed and dressed with the feeling that execution was imminent. Her mouth and eyes felt dry and gritty, and she had slept badly. She had made such a determined effort to be cheerful the previous evening that reaction had set in.

The stranger was coming at ten. At nine-thirty Alison forced a cup of black coffee down. Her stomach rebelled at the thought of anything more. She found the tension of waiting unbearable, and at half past nine told her mother she would take Rusty for a walk in the grounds.

As they set off she looked back to see the house, grand and immovable, facing the loch with the calm serenity it had had ever since the day it was built. A lump came into her throat. Her father had been born in that house, and his forefathers before him, and both

Alec and Alison herself. It was unthinkable to even consider letting it go, but barring a miracle, they had no choice.

Alison and Rusty walked slowly along, for the dog was old, and not interested in anything more than a gentle amble through the trees, with much sniffling and snuffling at interesting smells in the thick undergrowth. Alison had no particular destination in mind, but perhaps because of the memories revived the previous day, she found herself going towards the old trout stream which was already faintly to be heard in the distance as a murmuring whisper. Thin shafts of sunlight pierced the thick greenery overhead, and the entire wood had an aura of warm greenness, as if underwater. It was a strange, unusual atmosphere, slightly eerie, and her heart began to beat faster as she neared the stream. In a minute now she would see the clearing where that awful, fateful night . . .

She came past the final obstructing tree, and gasped, her hand going to her mouth in utter horror at the sight of the ghost who stood looking at the water. Then he turned, and it was no phantom, but a solid, flesh and blood man, larger and more confident than the last time she had seen him in just the same spot. The same place, the same person, but nine years after – Niall MacBain. And he stood watching her, waiting. Almost as if he had known she would come.

CHAPTER TWO

ALISON walked slowly towards him, motioning a curious Rusty to her side. Her first childish impulse was to shout: 'Go away!' but she was no longer a child. Nothing, however, could make her welcome him, and as she neared him, she said: 'What are you doing here?'

'Just looking, and thinking.' His voice was disconcerting, as was the expression in his eyes. In those few words, and the way he said them, was a world of difference from the rough, quick-tempered boy Alison remembered. This was a man, and fully aware of it. His hair was different, his face, and eyes, all so devastatingly masculine as to be an affront to her peace of mind. She was, after all, facing a trespasser, yet it was difficult to keep calm in the face of those disconcerting eyes, raking her from head to toe, subtly appraising her. It stung Alison to retort:

'You still enjoy trespassing?'

'You're mistaken – Miss Mackay.' The pause was deliberate, and faintly insulting. It made her feel curiously on the defensive.

He went on: 'I'm here by invitation.' His voice was soft.

'Invitation? Never! I wouldn't—' Alison stopped, seeing his smile. And still she didn't realize.

'Your mother's. Did she not tell you?'

'No! It – you c-can't.' She was stammering, and took a deep breath to steady herself. Now was the time for self-control. If the nightmare words he was saying were true, it meant that he was the 'stranger' who was coming to see her home.

She said more calmly: 'Are you telling me that you are the person who wants to buy Courthill?'

'I am.' He looked at his watch. 'I set off earlier than I intended, so decided to walk this way to the house. It seemed the natural thing to do, and after all, it will save you showing me round the grounds if I've already seen them, won't it?' There was a gleam of mockery in the dark grey eyes that touched a raw nerve in Alison.

'I'm sure you already know every inch of them,' she retorted. The shock had not subsided. A kind of dismay had her in its grip. Now she knew why her mother had been so distressed the previous night. Mrs. Mackay had been frightened of Alison's reaction, nervous that she would be angry. It was too soon, and the shock was too great for that – yet. Anger would come later. Just at the moment all she felt was a sick numbness. She watched as if in a dream as Rusty ambled over to him. The dog half wagged her tail, unsure whether he was friend or foe, until he stooped and patted her head, after letting her sniff his hand. As the tail wag increased rapidly, Alison called: 'Rusty, come here, girl!' And Niall looked up, the corner of his mouth quirking slightly. Unable to stand there a moment longer, Alison turned away and began to walk back home. Perhaps it was a bad dream. Perhaps he'll vanish if I ignore him completely, she thought wildly.

She heard footsteps behind her, his voice saying: 'It's nearly ten. I'll come to Courthill now.' And something snapped inside her. Whirling round, seeing him only inches away, she said:

'The joke's over. You've had your fun, now go. *You* buy my house? I'd rather die!'

A muscle tightened in his cheek, a dangerous sign that should have warned her. But his voice was quite calm as he answered softly: 'It's for your mother to say yes or no – not you.'

Then Alison said the unforgivable. Looking straight into his eyes, she retaliated with: 'She wants to *sell* it, not give it away. For money – if you know what that is!'

Under the tan, his face went white with anger, but she was beyond caring. Recklessly she spat out: 'So don't think you can waste our time. All you want to do is gloat over our misfortune.' Her eyes sparked fire, her fists were clenched tightly for control.

'For your information, I have the money to buy Courthill – and enough over to do all that's necessary to it. If what I hear about your home is true, it's certainly been allowed to deteriorate these last few years. Your spirited defence of it might be more credible if you'd taken the trouble to maintain it properly.'

Alison felt as if he had struck her. The hammer blow of each word struck more forcibly because of the expression in his eyes. She was helpless in the face of it, more so because she knew instinctively that he spoke the truth. There was superb confidence in his bearing, in his manner, in everything about him; the confidence that comes from wealth. She should have known, for it made even greater the contrast between the young aggressive fighter she remembered, and the man he was now. His temper was equally fiery, but clearly well under control, yet as she watched him, she felt fear. He would be a formidable opponent because of all these factors. Losing her own control would only do her harm she knew. She took a deep breath, fighting for calm.

'If it's in such poor condition, why are you interested?'

'I've always been interested, all my life. I made up my mind, even before I left home, that when I made a fortune, and the house came up for sale, I would buy it. I've made — not a fortune, but enough — and Courthill is now on the market, so—' he shrugged. 'I want to buy.'

'S-suppose my mother refuses to sell?' Alison lifted her chin defiantly.

He lifted one eyebrow fractionally. 'Why should she? You can't afford to live here any more. My money is as good as anybody's. She'll sell.'

'Perhaps not to *you*.'

'And how many more do you think you'll have interested, eh? I'll tell you — none! Beggars can't be choosers,' he finished cruelly.

Alison flinched. 'How dare you say that!'

'I haven't even started yet. And I'd need to go far before I could be as appallingly rude as you.' He was still angry. She could feel it, and there was something more that she didn't understand. It was as if, somehow, he was actually enjoying himself. Alison knew she could only make things worse, so she turned away. 'Come on, Rusty.' She began walking home, and there was silence behind her. Before the clearing vanished completely, she had an overwhelming, irresistible urge to turn round. He stood there, perfectly still, tall and erect. And he was watching her.

'What are we going to do, Jessie?' Alison implored her, watching the old woman as she bustled about the kitchen preparing lunch.

'What can we do, child?' Jessie answered. 'Your mother, bless her, has no choice.' She looked up from her pastry rolling. 'You should be away in there with them, you know.'

Alison shook her head. 'I couldn't, truly. I don't want to even speak to him, let alone sit in there drinking coffee like old friends. I'd throw it all over him, saucer and all, or be sick!'

'Aye,' Jessie gave her little smile. 'You always did have your share of the Mackay temper.' She shook her head wonderingly. 'Ach, but he's grown up into a good-looking devil, I'll say that. So dark, just like his father was as a young man.'

'Good-looking!' Alison nearly spilt her coffee. 'He's hateful, like a – a pirate! Black Niall, they used to call him. It suits him more than ever now. He's loathsome.'

'You think so? Aye well, maybe you're right. But you cannot deny he's a powerful figure of a man. He'll have broken a few hearts in his travels round the world, I'd wager.'

Something struck Alison, and she asked: 'Jessie, how do you think he's made enough money to buy our house? He's been in the Merchant Navy all these years, hasn't he?'

'That he has. And as for the money, it's as much a mystery to me as it is to you. I've heard nothing at all in the village, and that's unusual, but then the old man has never been one to talk about his sons.'

The faint jangle of the bell in the corner made the

two of them look at one another. Jessie said quietly: 'That's for you, lassie. Your mother said she'd ring when she needed you.'

Alison stood up and smoothed her skirt, suddenly nervous. It was frightening. She was in her own house, where she had lived all her life, and yet she was shaking at the thought of going into her own sitting-room to face a man she disliked. The worst aspect of it was the awful feeling of helplessness that filled her.

She walked across the hall and opened the door. Her mother was sitting on the settee by the fireplace. Dressed simply in cream sweater and brown skirt, she was a small appealing figure. Alison felt a surge of pity that her mother should be reduced to being nice to this awful man because of their financial situation, then she looked reluctantly at him standing by the window, gazing out. He turned at that moment, and their eyes met in silent hostility across the room.

'Alison dear,' her mother held out her hand to Alison, and she clasped it, dismayed to feel the fine tremor. So she too was nervous! 'I'd like you to show Mr. MacBain around the house and grounds—'

'Mother—' Alison began, agonized.

'Please, Alison.' The pressure of her hand increased slightly, and Alison subsided. 'Very well. Now?' She looked at him.

He inclined his head slightly. 'If that is convenient for you, Mrs. Mackay.' Alison might not have been there.

'Of course.' Her mother gave him a smile, but it looked strained, and Alison felt a quick rush of temper. What had he been saying to her? she wondered. Had he been bullying her?

'Are you all right, Mother?' she asked quietly.

'Perfectly, dear. I just want a little time to think.'

About what? Alison wondered. Before she could lose the resolve, she turned back to the dark silent man. 'Will you wait in the hall, please? I'll be with you in a moment.'

He went out, moving quietly and easily across the room, and without a word. As the door closed behind him Alison knelt down. 'Tell me quickly. Has he been awkward? Is he trying to force the price down?'

Her mother shook her head, fine lines round her eyes emphasizing the delicacy of her features. 'No, Alison, it's nothing – at all. He's not said a word out of place. I just have to consider things for a wee while. I'll tell you later, I promise. And please, dear, for my sake, try not to make it so very obvious that you dislike him.'

'You don't expect me to hold hands while I'm showing him round, do you?' Alison asked bitterly.

'I don't think he'd expect that,' Mrs. Mackay gave her a little smile, more herself. 'But be civil. He's not as bad as you think.'

He is infinitely worse, Alison thought, but she said nothing.

'All right, I'll try. Do – do you think he'll buy?'

Her mother nodded. 'Yes, I think he will. I'm sorry, but there it is. I'd be very foolish to turn him down.'

Alison went unsteadily to the door.

She hadn't realized how shabby the house was until she saw it through the eyes of a stranger. As they went through each of the seven bedrooms she saw him glance round, saw his hard incisive look as he examined windows, floors and walls, taking in everything, and she was filled with shame. That this day should come was bad enough, but to know that he was examining every crack and crevice, and filing it away in his mind, was humiliating too.

He brought a small book from his jacket pocket, and began making notes as they went along. Alison was too choked up to speak, only managing the briefest of comments as they went in each room. The beds in the unoccupied ones, sheeted and ghostly, were a reminder of days long gone, and the faded elegance of the high-ceilinged corridor upstairs seemed to hold the echoes of laughing voices as they walked along it.

She paused at the foot of the twisting, uncarpeted staircase to the attics. 'Do you want to see the small rooms upstairs?' she asked.

'If it's no trouble.' There was a hardness about him as he stood there waiting for her to lead the way up. Alison shivered inwardly. It was no use, she thought wryly, seeing his face. He had won.

The accumulated rubbish of many years lay in those sloping-ceilinged rooms. Boxes and trunks, piles of magazines, cases of books too precious to throw away, but too numerous for the library downstairs; and an old rocking horse that had been an integral part of the nursery, all reminders of the past, lay in the first of the five large attics. Alison looked around, realizing that everything would have to go. There would be no room in the cottage for any of it. Niall seemed oblivious of the clutter, striding over objects to reach the window and look out.

'Hm, I think these will do,' he was speaking to himself, and she wondered what he meant. He turned to her. 'How many more attics are there?'

'Four,' she answered. 'All the same as this.'

He wrote something down. 'Right. I'll see them some other time. We can go down now.' He came back towards Alison, and they went out. His words had puzzled her. There had been an expression on his face almost of satisfaction, as he had looked round the attic – as if confirming something he wanted to know. But what? Nobody, unless they had lots of children, or servants, could possibly need attics. As far as Alison was aware, he was possessed of neither – but then he was a man of mystery.

She took him through all the downstairs rooms, save the one where her mother sat with Rusty. When she took him into the conservatory he nodded approvingly. 'This is fine – very interesting. Who looks after all these plants?' His gesturing arm took in the green wilderness of potted plants all around them, the ivies and cyclamens, a tall philodendron that curled all over the glass roof, threatening to take over, and the various cacti and succulents that Alison tended so carefully in her spare time.

'I do,' she answered briefly. 'I'll show you the studio. This way, please.'

A passage led off from the conservatory, with its permanently damp earthy smell, and they walked along stone flags to Alison's favourite room. This, her mother's studio, was a large, airy stone-built shed that had been added to the side of the house years ago. Almost all windows, the light, and the views, were exhilarating. Paintings were propped against the walls and chairs, and on the easel was one, not yet dry, of the loch at night. Niall stopped in front of it, and looked backing slightly to get it into better perspective. Alison

36

wanted to pull him away to prevent him seeing something so intensely personal. But she had to stand there, her hand gripping the door handle so tightly that her knuckles were white with strain. She felt physically exhausted with the stress of resisting all the natural primitive urges to send him away. He looked at her after a few minutes.

'Now, may we go outside?'

'You've seen the gardens before,' she answered stiffly.

'But not properly. Mainly at night.' A slight, mocking smile lit his face briefly, and was gone. 'I would like to see round in daylight. And the garages, and the chapel, of course.'

Alison looked sharply at him. 'That hasn't been used for years.'

'I'd still like to see it – if I may.' The last three words left no doubt of his intention to get his own way. She shrugged, and he opened the door for her to go out before him.

The nightmare was over half an hour later when they went back into the house. The tension and strain had left Alison feeling so weak that she stumbled over the bottom step as she went up to the front door. Immediately he shot out a hand to steady her, and the touch was like fire on her arm. She regained her balance and moved quickly away. 'Thank you.'

'A pleasure.' A warm rush of colour surged into her face at the mocking words. He hated her as much as she did him, she already sensed. She wondered if he remembered the incident after the dance nine years ago, and as she did, recalled his last words, spoken in temper, of 'taking her down a peg or two.'

37

Could this be it? His revenge, cruel and subtle? Alison looked quickly at him as she opened the front door, and their eyes clashed for one awful moment. The look in his made her shiver; a look of suppressed, smouldering anger. She took a deep breath, suddenly afraid. If this was his way of doing it, he was choosing a superbly refined way of torture. One that would go on and on; for as long as she lived, Alison knew she would not forget the man who was depriving her of her home.

Alison had thought that nothing could be worse, or more distressing than having to show Niall MacBain round her home. She was wrong. It happened after they returned to the room where her mother waited. Mrs. Mackay looked up – at him, not at Alison – and something passed between them, some unspoken question. Alison glanced quickly at Niall.

'Have you said anything?' her mother asked him. He shook his head.

'No, I thought it would be better if you did that, Mrs. Mackay.'

'What is it?' Alison's heart began to pound.

'Wait, Alison. First, Mr. MacBain, you've seen round now. Does your offer still stand?'

He walked slowly from the door to Mrs. Mackay, then stood in front of her. 'Yes, Mrs. Mackay, it does. Say the word and we'll go to the solicitor's on Monday.'

'Mother, before you say another thing, please – what should he have told me?' Alison was breathless, as if she had been running. She knew that in another moment a final irrevocable act would take place; a handshake of agreement.

Her mother looked at her almost sadly. 'Mr. Mac-Bain is going to turn Courthill into a hotel.'

'Oh, no!' Alison closed her eyes, shocked beyond measure, seeing him again looking round the chapel, nodding approvingly, saying: 'This could be repaired quite easily.' And in the attic too ... Now she knew why. Her home, a hotel, with loud strangers walking in and out as if they owned it, going out in boats from the private mooring, walking through the woods, fishing ...

'No, you can't do it! Don't let him!' She looked at him standing there, and for the first time in her life, wished that she were a man. She wanted to knock him senseless, to fight him, punish him in the only way he understood, by brute force. Almost shaking, she said: 'Don't sell to him, Mother. We'll find someone else—' and he turned and looked at her, and she saw a puzzling expression, almost of pity. A second later it was gone, to be replaced by studied blankness, as he said: 'Perhaps I should go out for a while if you wish to discuss it?'

'That won't be necessary,' said her mother. 'Alison, calm yourself, I beg you.' Alison sat down beside her, wanting so much to cry, holding herself in check by a strong effort of will. Of course she could do nothing. Her mother had already decided. That was what she had wanted to think over when they had gone out. And there was worse to come. Much worse. But Alison didn't find out what it was until later in the day.

She watched their handshake. Then her mother said: 'Sit down, please, Mr. MacBain. There are one or two things we must discuss.'

He sat down opposite them, and Rusty ambled over and collapsed at his feet in a pleading heap, her tail wagging. He bent and began to scratch her ears idly as he said: 'The cottage you wish to live in. Is that the one by the loch?'

'Yes. It's quite separate, and I dare say we could fence off a path to the main road.'

'As you like, though it's immaterial to me. You may use the grounds as you please.' He paused, then added: 'And, Mrs. Mackay, your studio – I wouldn't want to take that from you. If you want to continue using it, it's yours.'

Alison heard her mother's sharp, disbelieving intake of breath, then: 'Why, that's – very kind of you. Are you sure—?'

'Quite sure. We can easily make a door in the studio itself, and block off the one from the conservatory, so that no guests will stray. You'll have your own key, of course.'

'Thank you. There really wouldn't be room at the cottage. I was wondering what on earth I would do.'

You'd think he was doing her a great honour, Alison thought bitterly.

'And the island, Mrs. Mackay. When may I see the island?'

'Mother! You're not selling the island too?' Alison gasped.

Her mother looked at her. 'Of course. It goes with the house, dear, you know that. Besides, what use would it be to us?'

'I often go, and you're always painting there—'

'I'm sure Mr. MacBain wouldn't mind us going.' She turned to him. 'The views from it are magnificent.

Quite inspiring for a painter.'

'I'm sure.' He smiled at her. 'I might repair the cottage on it – perhaps rent it out as a honeymoon island—'

'How romantic!' Mrs. Mackay clasped her hands to her breast. Alison looked stonily at him. His eyes had flickered towards her as he had said the words almost mockingly. By now she was nearly past caring. She didn't think anything else could happen to affect her. She found out how wrong she was later.

'Alison will take you there this afternoon,' said her mother.

'You know your own way there, don't you, Mr. MacBain? I'm sure you'll manage better on your own,' Alison said, knowing she was being appallingly rude.

'I would prefer you to take me,' he answered calmly. 'After all, you know your own boat best, and I'd hate to damage it.'

Her mother looked doubtfully at them both, fully aware of the charged atmosphere, and torn with indecision. Alison stood up.

'I'll take you. And now, if you'll excuse me, I have a lot of work to do.' She went out quickly and shut the door behind her. Her destination was the kitchen, there to pour out her feelings to Jessie. She would understand, especially about the island, more than her mother who, in the last few minutes, had seemed almost visibly to go over to the enemy side. It was, thought Alison in horror, almost as if she *liked* him.

Under any other circumstances the boat ride to the island at the mouth of the loch would have been enjoyable. It was a warm afternoon, laced with a stiff breeze,

41

and the boat sped across the calm deep loch with scarcely any effort at all. Alison sat in the bows and watched them cleave through the black waters, but her heart was heavy. She looked back to see her home and the village receding rapidly. It was a beautiful sight, only spoiled by the man leaning against the stern, hand on tiller as he guided them along.

He had returned after lunch, having changed into thick white sweater, grey leather jacket, and tight-fitting grey slacks. Binoculars were slung on a long cord round his neck. The sweater accentuated his tan, and the jacket matched his eyes, and if Alison hadn't loathed him so deeply, she would have admitted that Jessie's assessment, 'a good-looking devil,' was an almost perfect way to describe him. He was over six feet tall, towering easily over her; long-legged, slim-hipped, and broad-shouldered. So that was what life in the Navy had done for him, she thought; turned him into a tough-looking giant. But how had he made his so-called fortune?

Alison turned away, her eye caught by the shiny black shape that heaved itself up out of the water, then vanished. A seal most likely, or a porpoise. Both were quite common in the warm summer months, and curious enough to go near a boat to see what it was.

Niall and Alison hadn't spoken since they had left the house. She had nothing to say to him, nor he apparently to her.

She looked over to the distant schoolroom, now smaller than a matchbox, and thought with bitterness how only two days ago she had wondered whose was the stranger's car. Her premonition had been right. The car that had carried Niall MacBain back home to

Shielbaig had brought trouble with it.

They were nearly there. Alison turned back again to see the island looming before them, spreading and widening as they came into its shadow. It wasn't large, a quarter of a mile long, and the same width, in a very rough square shape. It was big enough to have deep caves, and plentiful trees and shrubs, and a cottage, the roof of which was faintly visible through the trees as Alison bent to see where the treacherous underwater rocks were.

'Left a bit,' she called, and felt the surge left as they coasted gently in, bumping a bit in the waves that lapped against the shingly shore. Niall switched the motor off and it put-puttered into silence. There was only the creak of the wood as the boat's keel touched the gravelly beach. Niall came swiftly past Alison, jumped out and pulled the boat up on to the shore.

Before he could offer her his arm, Alison jumped out too, glad that she'd worn wellingtons instead of shoes, with her outfit of rust-coloured sweater and pants. Their footsteps crunched on thousands of tiny shells and pebbles, and Niall looked around him appraisingly.

'Marvellous.' He turned to her. 'Don't you think so?'

'Yes,' she answered briefly. 'Where do you want to go first?'

He gave her an odd, very level look. 'The cottage, I think.'

Alison shrugged. 'As you wish.'

'Can you manage the climb? Do you want help?' he asked.

'From you?' she looked at him, not bothering to con-

43

ceal her feelings. 'No, thank you. I can manage.'

There was silence for a moment, then he said slowly, with a hard cutting edge to his voice: 'Let's get one thing straight. If you think you can, by your childish and silly behaviour, make me back out of buying Courthill, you're very much mistaken. In fact, it only makes me more determined to have it.'

'Does it?' She faced him then, her breathing fast, as if she had been running. 'Or had you already made up your mind years ago? You've chosen a cruel way to have your revenge, haven't you? Oh, don't think I don't know. I remember.'

He looked puzzled. 'Revenge? What the hell are you talking about?'

'Don't look so innocent. I have a good memory.'

'Better than mine, it seems,' he stared steadily at her, and his eyes were like chips of granite. 'You'd better tell me.'

So she reminded him of the words he had spoken at the end of the evening nine years before, and when she finished, he nodded.

'So that's what's biting you?' he gave a wry smile. 'And you think that something I said in temper – I was in a temper too – would make me alter my life, just to have revenge on a girl? My God, but you're more foolish than I thought.' And for a moment she believed him – almost.

She turned towards the rocks to begin the climb to the cottage. Anything to get away from him. She was seething at his manner, the way he had an answer for everything. He had always been the same, arrogant and sure. Now, the only difference was that he had the appearance to go with it. No longer the boy in ill-fitting

44

hand-me-downs, perpetually shabby, but now the man, so well dressed and assured that it seemed to her he could get away with anything he chose. He had already won her mother over. It was a fact Alison had to face. And Rusty too, dear old Rusty, she thought. Who next? she wondered bitterly as she scrambled up the rocky track to the cottage. Not Jessie, surely? She shivered, afraid. It would be unbearable to be entirely alone with no one to tell, to confide in. Alison had a dear friend, Meg, living near Inverness. But even with her it would not be the same, for she could not know of the emotions that had built up over the years, smouldering hatreds fanned by all the incidents through childhood, and now, years later, brought to the point of explosion by this one man. No one could understand, except Alec, and he was too far away to do anything. Married with two children, he worked on a hydro-electric scheme in Canada's icy north. He would feel as Alison did about his home going to Niall MacBain, especially when she told him that it would be opened as a hotel.

As her fingers scrabbled for a handhold on the roughest part of the path, her foot dislodged a stone that went bowling down. She turned instinctively to shout, but too late. Even as she did, she saw the piece of rock land squarely on Niall's hand as he held on to a hummock of grass, and then the blood spurted out and she turned away, sick and faint.

At the top, she leaned over to help him the last few feet, but he ignored her outstretched hand, whipped a handkerchief from his pocket, and bound it quickly round his left hand.

'I'm sorry,' she said. 'It was an accident.'

'Was it?' He gave her a smouldering look and began to walk towards the cottage that was visible through the trees. Alison ran to catch up with him, sick with regret for what, after all, had been a genuine accident, yet stirred to anger by the utter contempt in his voice.

'Yes, it was.' She caught up with him at last. 'You must have seen me going up. I couldn't have fore-seen—'

'Forget it,' he cut in, and stopped walking to look down at her. 'You've been up that track enough times to know the dangers of loose rocks and stones, I'm sure. And to know how to avoid dislodging them. Instead, though, you charge up like a child of five, with no sense of danger—'

'If you're so clever,' she was stung to retort, keeping her eyes averted from the widening patch of red in the white handkerchief, 'why didn't you wait until I reached the top before setting off?'

'Because you looked as if you'd fall, the way you were going. Better to catch you half way than to let you roll all the way down.'

Alison's eyes blazed back into his. 'I would have thought you'd be only too pleased if I had!'

'My intentions are to buy your house, not to kill you off,' he replied softly, with ice in his voice. Something warned Alison not to go any further, an inner voice telling her what she already knew, that this man's patience was dangerously near breaking point.

She drew a deep breath, unable to take her eyes from his face, lean and attractive, slightly pale now, but whether from pain or anger, she did not know.

'Would you like to go back, and see the island

tomorrow?' she asked quietly.

'No. Why?' He looked down at his hand. 'I've had worse than this. I dare say I'll survive.'

'I have another hanky somewhere,' she began.

'It doesn't matter.' He walked on and left her standing there. When she reached the cottage which was set in a clearing, the stone walls still firm, and the corrugated iron roof bright orange with rust, he was walking slowly round it, looking up and down as if visualizing it when repaired. Then he went in, and Alison waited.

It was coming to her that she was fighting a losing battle against this formidable man. Would it not be better, she reflected, as she saw him pass a window, if she just let everything happen? It seemed inevitable that the sale would go through. Her mother would be foolish to refuse a cash offer. They had no money to stay on there, and even a hotel would be better than seeing their once lovely home deteriorate rapidly, as it soon would. Alison loved it so dearly, yet was not blind to its defects, nor did she expect a miracle. This was probably the best chance they would ever have. Perhaps, when it was finished he would go away, leaving someone else in charge. He was a seaman, they seldom settled easily to land. It might be possible to forget, again . . .

'I'm going to look round. Coming?' His voice was a harsh intrusion into her thoughts.

Numbly she nodded. He had insisted on her presence. She might as well see it herself while they were there – see what they were losing. I'm growing sentimental, she thought wryly, as they scrambled down through the thick pines, with the strong tangy scent all around them. Descent was easier on the south side of the island. She should have remembered that, but her thoughts had been chaotic since his arrival that morning. It was not surprising that she had forgotten the obvious. Alison watched him as he went nimbly down ahead of her, never once looking behind him, or offering to help. His back was straight, his shoulders broad. A powerful and determined man, and so vastly different from the boy she had known and loathed, that she could still scarcely believe it. And yet could she not admit it at last? Under the dislike, mingling with it even, had there not been some trace of admiration for such a free, reckless spirit as he? Frightened of nothing, going anywhere he chose and getting himself in and out of trouble the only way he knew – with his fists. Was there not an element of devilry there that had fined down, become tempered in the man? And did it not make him more worthy of attention because of that? Reluctantly, Alison admitted the truth of her thoughts. And knew too, in that moment of revelation, that if he opened a hotel, it would be a good one. There would be nothing second rate for Niall MacBain.

He reached the stony shore and partly turned, waiting for her.

'This way.' He set off in a westward direction, and Alison followed. This was perhaps the best side of the island, for from the beach they could see Skye in the distance, with the ghostly grey-blue sweep of the Cuillins, mistily beckoning yet seemingly unapproachable. Alison stood still, looking at them with the sense of wonder that always possessed her.

Niall turned impatiently and she hurried after him. The day was a terrible one, and she wanted to go home. She shivered. He wanted this island, this small wooded piece of land at the mouth of the loch. She felt as if he were trying to take everything away from her; all the security she had known in her life seemed to be crumbling away like fine sand washed by the sea. And soon all they would have left would be the small cottage that had once belonged to the gardener and his family. And the studio – she had almost forgotten that. Why had he made such an apparently generous gesture?

As they came to the jutting out rocks on the far west of the island, he stopped and put the binoculars to his eyes as he gazed towards Skye. And Alison decided to ask.

'Why have you let my mother keep her studio?' she said bluntly.

The binoculars wavered, then he turned and looked at her. He lifted a quizzical eyebrow. 'Don't you ever try a little subtlety in your cross-examinations?' Alison felt herself go pink, for a gleam of amusement lit his dark face.

'I don't think you appreciate subtlety,' she replied. 'I've not been aware of any in *your* behaviour so far.'

'True,' he shrugged, and turned away, lifting the glasses again to his eyes. Then casually he asked: 'Do I have to have a reason?'

'Yes, I think you do,' she answered, keeping her voice level. 'But I can't see what it is.'

'No, you wouldn't.' He lowered the glasses, and made as if to take them from his neck. 'Do you want to look?'

'No, thank you.' He was going to tell her something,

she knew. She wanted no distractions.

'Very well. It's quite simple. Your mother used to be an interior designer. I want her to help me plan the layout and decor of the hotel.'

So that was it! Alison gave a disbelieving laugh. 'And do you honestly think she will? You must be mad!'

'You think so?' he answered softly. 'Why?'

'Because she feels like me. She won't want anything to do with you once we've sold Courthill. You must be very insensitive to expect otherwise!' she retorted. 'And you thought you'd bribe her by letting her keep the studio. When I tell her, she'll fling it back at you!'

'On the contrary,' he smiled slightly. It was almost as if he was enjoying himself, and perhaps it should have warned her. 'That's where you're mistaken. I've already asked her – before I thought about the studio – and she has agreed. Your mother, Miss Mackay, is going to be working for me!'

CHAPTER THREE

THAT night, for the first time in years, Alison cried herself to sleep. The nightmare was endless. Niall Mac-Bain, for all his protestations to the contrary, was exacting a subtle and terrible revenge against his family's old enemies. And Alison seemed to be trapped in the middle of a giant web, unable to free herself, seeing herself getting more tangled with every slight effort to get free.

After Niall's awful words, she had walked away and gone back to the boat to wait alone for him to finish his tour of the island. She no longer wanted to speak to him, or have to look at him.

When they landed she had gone straight into the house, leaving him to secure the boat. That too would soon be his, she thought, as she made her angry way to Courthill. She couldn't even face her mother, for she knew she might say things she would regret. Instead she went straight upstairs after telling Jessie she had a headache, and was going to lie down. Something about Jessie's face made her want to break down and cry, there and then in the kitchen. But she managed to resist.

On Sunday she got up early and packed a picnic lunch. She wanted time alone, to think, and the best way was to find somewhere quiet, far away, with only Rusty for company. She got home late, tired but still no clearer in her mind, and went straight to bed.

Her mother, so Jessie told her, had been working all

day in the studio.

Next morning Alison breakfasted alone. It was her mother's turn to have a headache, apparently. Alison didn't even know how long Niall had stayed, or what had been said, on Saturday. She preferred not to know.

As she passed the MacBain house on her way to school, it was the hardest thing to keep looking ahead. It was as if a magnet drew her eyes to the tiny house. The car was standing outside, so Niall was at home. Alison wondered if he had told his father everything, and felt her throat become constricted. How the old man would chuckle! He had always hated them, even more than his four sons. Revenge must be that much sweeter for him. She blinked furiously, for a sharp breeze blew specks of sand into her eyes, stinging them. Whatever happened, she must not let any of her feelings show in front of the class, for they were bright youngsters, alert to the slightest sign of anything out of the ordinary, and if she wasn't careful, she knew it would be all round the village that 'Miss' was upset.

She managed to put everything to one side, and concentrate on the work. She even managed to run down the hill with the children at lunchtime, so that as she ran through the woods towards home, flushed and breathless, her troubles were nearly forgotten.

Then she saw the car stopping outside the front door as she went towards it, and she slowed down. Niall MacBain got out, and opened the front passenger door for Alison's mother, who seeing her, said:

'Heavens, is it that time already?' and looking at him, added: 'Will you come in for a coffee?'

'No, thanks, Mrs. Mackay.' He was watching Alison

steadily. 'I'll away home now. I'm going to Inverness later, and won't be back until Thursday. Is it all right if I come round then?'

'Yes, of course. Goodbye, Mr. MacBain.'

Alison turned away and ran up the steps. A moment later her mother followed, and as she shut the door, they heard the car go down the drive.

Before Alison could speak, her mother said: 'Why are you so rude to him?' Alison looked incredulously at her. She was watching Alison with a puzzled look on her face. Stunned, Alison answered: 'Rude? I can barely look at him, let alone speak. He's taking our home away from us, and our island – and you – even you, Mother. You're going t-to work for him, aren't you? Why, oh, why?'

Mrs. Mackay nodded. 'He told me about it. I would have preferred to explain to you myself, but there—' she pulled a little face. 'I'm sorry, darling, but how can I turn down good money, tell me that?'

'We're not that desperate,' Alison muttered. 'And there'll be his money for the house—'

'Don't you see?' her mother was genuinely upset. 'I love this old place as much as you. Oh, Alison, if I can, by my effort and designs, bring it to life again, even if for others, it will be worth it. He has the money to spend. I'd be foolish to let someone else decide what colours for this room, or the hall or the bedrooms, when I who know them so well can plan the colours and everything else.' She looked round and lifted her arms wide in a sweeping gesture. 'Can't you see it all?'

Alison nodded reluctantly, glad that she hadn't approached her before. They would both have regretted it. Yet it was frightening how logical each move of his could be made to seem.

'I'm sorry, Mother,' she said. 'But I just feel as if he's taking everything away from me.'

Mrs. Mackay looked at her, and compassion shone in her eyes. 'Oh, darling, you mustn't think like that. He's not wicked. There's something very – well, nice about him. I can't explain it.' She smiled. 'Dear me, I'd better not let him hear, had I? We've been to the solicitor's, by the way.'

'I guessed that. So it's definite, is it?' Alison's heart twisted inside her. He had cast a spell over her mother.

'Almost. There are the usual legal proceedings to be gone through, of course, but they won't take long, two or three weeks at most. And then the house will belong to him.'

'And we will leave it,' Alison said softly.

'Yes. It will be difficult at first, I know, but we'll soon settle in.' She took Alison's arm. 'Come away, we'll see what Jessie has for lunch, and then you must get back to your bairns.'

The week dragged by. On Thursday when Alison returned home from school at four, there was a little man from the County Council, going round with steel measure and notebook. He gave Alison a slow smile and politely tipped his hat, assuring her with grave Highland courtesy that he'd be 'no sort of a nuisance at all.'

She was sufficiently interested in what sort of plans that Niall had for her home that she asked him if she could watch him at work. He seemed pleased at her interest, clearly mistaking it, and she left him with the wrong impression, hoping thereby to discover more.

A picture came over as they went along of what exactly Niall had in mind. There was to be no massive resculpting of Courthill, in fact he didn't intend to touch the exterior, but inside most of the larger bedrooms were to be halved, and as in each case they had more than one window, there would be no difference outside. A small room on the first floor was to be made into a bathroom, as was one of the attics. The only thing that would show on the outside was a fire escape from the top floor to the ground, but the little man assured Alison it would be at the side of the house, and scarcely visible at all. He spoke knowledgeably of gable ends and plasterboard, and damp courses, and Alison nodded and hoped that her lamentable ignorance didn't show.

When he had finished, she saw him to the door. He made it clear that there would be no difficulty in the planning permission coming through, and it was with a heavy heart that she bade him goodbye. Soon there would be an end to their peaceful existence. The place would echo to the sound of hammers on wood, and the tramp of heavy boots on bare boards. And it would never be the same, ever again.

She went along to her mother's studio and knocked.

'Come in.' Her mother looked up, focusing her eyes to the present from the world she occupied when painting. 'Has he gone?'

Alison nodded, and her mother smiled at her. 'Good. I couldn't bear to stay. Is it – is he going to do a lot to the house?'

Alison told her as well as she remembered, of the

alterations on all three floors, and when she had finished, her mother nodded, and gave a sigh of relief. 'Thank God! He's not going to ruin it.'

'Did you have doubts?' Alison asked curiously.

'No, but – well, one never knows.'

'It's still not too late,' Alison said quietly.

Her mother looked at her oddly. 'You really do hate him?'

'Yes, I do.'

Mrs. Mackay's eyes stayed on Alison's face. 'I've never seen you like this. I always thought you were too sensible to let a family feud go to such lengths, but I believe you meant what you just said. Why?'

Alison shook her head. Some things went too deep for words. She could no more have revealed her innermost feelings and fears than she could fly. Even to her mother, warm-hearted, understanding and loving, even to her it was impossible to explain the extreme aversion that she felt whenever Niall MacBain was near. She didn't want to try. Instead she answered: 'Perhaps it's in my blood, Mother. Like it was in Alec's, remember? Only he could fight it out – I can't.' She tried to laugh, to make light of it. 'Heavens, can you see me having a punch-up with Niall MacBain?'

But her mother didn't laugh. She looked down at the paint-covered palette she held, and she spoke softly, as if to herself. 'I think he'd be a difficult man to get on the wrong side of. Don't push him too far.'

'Are you warning me?' Alison pretended alarm, her eyes wide.

Her mother shook her head, a faint smile on her lips. 'Just giving you a motherly word of advice, Alison. I don't want to see you hurt. Men like him can be ruthless. He had a hard childhood, don't forget, and he's travelled the world since, and made money. That's a dangerous combination in any man. I sensed his vibrant power when I met him the other day. It's well concealed, but it's there all right – a hard core of steel beneath the velvet exterior. It's in his eyes and in his face – a remarkable face really, in one so young. I'd like to paint him some day.'

Alison heard a distant bell, the front door, and said: 'That may be him now. I'll away to see.' She turned and went out before her mother could see the effect of her words. They had disturbed Alison deeply, confirming what she already knew about him. He could be a dangerous enemy. But if her mother thought she would meekly acquiesce because of those words, then she didn't know her daughter as well as she apparently knew Niall MacBain, thought Alison wryly.

Jessie had let him in when she reached the hall. She was just saying: 'I'll fetch Mrs. Mackay,' when she heard Alison and turned.

'It's all right, Jessie,' Alison said with a warm smile. Then she looked at the waiting man, and removed the smile slowly. 'I'll take you to my mother, Mr. MacBain,' she said, 'if you'll follow me.'

'Thank you.' He gave Jessie a friendly nod, and Alison turned and started to go back the way she had come, leaving him to follow.

She walked steadily, feeling his eyes on her back, resisting a primitive urge to hit him, and wondering why he always made her feel so breathless, as if she had been running, whenever he was near.

She tapped on the door and opened it. 'Go in, Mr. MacBain.'

He looked straight into her eyes and she flinched at the cold greyness of them. But all he said was: 'Thank you.' He went in and she shut the door, her hand suddenly trembling as she turned the handle. As she moved away she heard him say: 'I've just now returned from Inverness, Mrs. Mackay. Did someone come . . .?' his voice faded as she walked quickly away, out of earshot. Alison knew now, partly anyway, why her mother found him so interesting. His voice just then, to her, had been full of warmth and charm. The perfect gentleman, she thought wryly as she made her way through the damp greenness of the plants in the conservatory. Perhaps when the house was his, and she was actually working for him, some of the charm might wear off, and her mother would see his true nature. But by then it would be too late. Much too late.

That evening Alison's mother told her that over the week-end Niall wanted to come to the house and measure up for all the wood and building materials that would be needed. Alison looked at her, aghast. 'And you said yes?'

'Of course. I'm sorry, darling, but there it is. You'll just have to keep out of the way.' As Alison nodded, her mother added: 'Look, why don't you phone your friend Meg? You've not seen her for ages, and she's always asking you down. See if she and Bill will put you up for the week-end.'

Alison looked at her. 'Of course! I'll phone her now. It'll be good to see her again,' and to tell her all about *him*, and get some of the growing heaviness off my chest, but she added that only inwardly. She prayed, as she dialled the number, that Meg wouldn't have decided to go camping with Bill and the children that week-end. Her prayers were answered. When she got through, and asked her question, Meg squealed with delight.

'Alison, of course. I'd love to see you. When? Friday evening? What time? And you're coming in the car? I can't wait!'

It was so nice to hear her friendly warm voice, and to know that there, at last, she would be able to talk freely. Alison came away from the phone with a light heart, planning what she would wear.

'Alison, he sounds *awful*! A veritable monster!' Meg watched her wide-eyed over the coffee cup she held. She shivered deliciously. 'I mean, it's too rich for words. I'm sure you're exaggerating!'

Alison laughed, happy for the first time in a week. It was Friday, nearly midnight, and she and Meg were sitting by the fire in her bungalow on the outskirts of Inverness. They were both in their dressing gowns, and held coffee cups, while outside the rain lashed mercilessly down. Nearby in one of the bedrooms slept Meg's three-year-old twin sons, in another her husband, Bill, kind and witty, who had told them as he bade them good night: 'I'll leave you girls to your gossiping – and please don't wake me with your giggling, or I might get cross –and I'm a tiger when I'm roused!'

That had started them off laughing at the thought, and somehow it had set the mood for their talk, and strangely enough, there in that warm room, Niall Mac-Bain and all he represented, seemed so far away as to be neutralized, until Alison almost felt as if she *were* exaggerating. Meg was the ideal confidant. The perfect listener, she never interrupted, and had listened agog from the beginning of Alison's tale until she finished with her mother's words of warning the previous afternoon.

Meg leaned over to refill their cups from the coffee pot in the fireplace. Alison watched her with affection, feeling much better than she had ever thought possible. They were both the same age, had studied at teacher training college in Edinburgh together, and Meg had gone to Dingwall after qualifying, Alison to Shielbaig. Meg had only been teaching a year when the new, handsome young sports teacher, Bill Graham, had swept her off her feet. They had married, Meg intending to go on teaching for several years, but Nature decided otherwise, and within a year of the wedding Alison had been godmother at the christening of their month-old twins. Meg was auburn-haired, calm-faced and, since the birth of her babies, slightly plump, which added to rather than detracted from her pleasant looks. They kept in touch by phone and letter, and many times Meg and her husband had gone to Courthill with a tent and camped in the woods for a week-end. They always firmly refused offers of beds in the house, but gratefully accepted Jessie's culinary hospitality, for Bill considered that she cooked like an angel, and insisted that he only came so that he could eat her fluffy scrambled eggs for breakfast!

Now Meg, having refilled Alison's cup, looked up, a glimmer of light dawning. 'MacBain? Didn't you once tell me something *awful* about him? Something happened after a dance, you know – and he gave a boy a black eye—'

'That's him!' Alison burst out. 'The family feud. So you see—'

'But quite frankly, I can't connect the two. Honestly, you remember how we used to talk it over in our room when we were at college, and to me it was almost – well, you know – romantic.'

She went a little pink at Alison's disbelieving gaze, and persisted: 'Yes, it was. You know, deadly enemies, but he rescues you from the clutches of a veritable wolf, then kisses you—' here she fluttered her eyelashes, – 'I mean, it's the sort of thing we used to love reading about when we were younger. Don't you remember, Alison?'

Alison did. She was silent for a moment, thinking of the pleasure the telling and retelling of the incident had given them both at college. Strangely, seen through Meg's eyes like that, Alison could appreciate her meaning. There *was* a romantic flavour about it. But now – she shivered and pulled closer to the fire.

'Well, Meg, you'd have to see him now to know what I mean. He's utterly different, obviously. There's something about him that's almost frightening.'

'Mmm, well,' Meg looked severely at Alison. 'I can see there's only one thing for it. I'll have to persuade Bill to load up the tent, and we'll sort of mosey along your way, and pitch camp for a few nights. Then I'll see for myself.'

'Would you? I believe you would!' Alison stared at her, then began to laugh. 'Oh, Meg, you do me good. Why don't we live nearer to one another?'

Meg smiled. 'Perhaps we can arrange to have Inverness moved a little closer to Shielbaig.'

The following Monday was cold and wet. The children were fractious, and Fiona Stewart, usually quiet, hit Willy MacLeod with a ruler and started a free-for-all that took Alison several minutes to quell. She sorted out their grievances, discovered that Fiona had caught Willy bullying one of the younger boys, and had exacted her own justice. By the time all was peaceful it was four o'clock, and Alison dismissed them, quite sure that the quarrel would break out afresh once they were away from the school.

She crossed to the window to see, and watched them run helter-skelter down the hill. A man stood aside to let them pass, a familiar figure . . . Alison's heart skipped a beat. It was Niall MacBain, and he seemed to be walking towards the school! He looked up, and must have seen her at the window. She was about to move away, almost guiltily, when she stopped herself. She had every right to be there, she decided. And so she waited. It was possible that he was going to one of the two houses that lay past the school. Possible, but highly improbable, for both were occupied by elderly single women who both owned lots of cats, and rarely spoke to anyone.

Alison moved back slightly as he looked up again, then chiding herself for silly curiosity, moved away and went to her desk. She tidied everything, found a rubber she had been searching for since the previous week, and then stood up. Her coat hung in the corner at the end of a row of pegs. A solitary unclaimed scarf was the only other occupant. She picked up her coat, put it on, and was about to go to the door, when it opened, and Niall MacBain walked slowly in.

'May I come in?' he asked.

'Yes,' she had to swallow. 'What do you want, Mr. MacBain?'

'To talk to you for a minute.' He spoke quietly, and Alison looked at the middle button on his jacket, for she knew what she would see if their eyes met, and she wasn't ready for that cold look, not yet. In a minute she would be, when the shock of his arrival had subsided.

She took a deep breath and slowly met his glance. 'I think anything you have to say is better said to my mother. You are dealing entirely with her. I'm sorry.'

'No,' he shook his head very slightly. 'This has nothing to do with Courthill. This is your business. School business.'

'I don't understand.' Alison's puzzlement showed on her face, and his own suddenly relaxed its serious expression as he said: 'I assure you this is no joke. I've merely come to see if you have room for another pupil. Have you?'

'Why, yes.' She hid her astonishment as best she could. 'There are only seven at the moment. Are – are you telling me you want to enrol a child?'

'I am.' He stood there watching her, and Alison turned away and went to her desk. She pulled out her large notebook, opened it, and pressed the page flat with her hand. And all the time that she did this, a sense of unreality filled her.

'May I have the child's name and age?' She looked up at him.

'Yes. André Luis Garcia. He's six years old.'

She wrote the name and the figure six, then said: 'And his address?'

'His present one doesn't matter. When he arrives here, he will be staying at my father's home in Sheilbaig, with me.'

'I see.' She wrote: 'Shielbaig, Strathcorran, Rossshire.' Then she looked up again. 'I gather he isn't British. May I know his nationality, and the length of time he'll be here?'

'He is Brazilian. He—' Niall paused, and Alison saw an odd expression on his face. He noted the glance, and looked slowly round the classroom. For a moment there was a tense silence, so taut that she feared to break it. Then he spoke again. 'He will be staying here for good. This is his new home.' His voice had gone harsh, as though it was an effort to speak.

'Thank you.' She carefully wrote: 'Permanent Resident.' Then closing the book, said: 'I'll have to inform the authorities, of course. When do you want him to start?'

'He's arriving Wednesday. Shall we say next Monday?'

'Very well – Monday.' She bit her lip. 'There's something I'd better tell you. The school may have to close after Christmas. There will be only two – or rather three pupils left. They will have to go to school in Strathcorran.'

He nodded. 'That's something that I'll worry about when the times comes. Meanwhile, he is booked in?'

'Yes, he is.'

His eyes went round the small room again, with its walls covered by the children's paintings and poems, and their plants on the windowsills. A friendly, homely room, it had changed little since the day twenty years previously that he had left. Even the desks were the same. Deeply scratched and scarred, the dark wood with a patina of age, they stood square and solid, having withstood the battering from dozens of small bodies, and elbows, and well aimed ink darts.

Alison wondered if the same memories were going through his mind. And at that moment he looked up, and his eyes, fractionally, had lost some of their hardness.

'Well, if that's all?' He made as if to move towards the door.

'Yes, it is. Except – oh yes, one more thing. I must know André's legal guardian.' She leaned over to pick up the book again.

And she waited. For a moment there was silence, then he said:

'I am.'

She swallowed. 'I see,' and began to write: 'Guardian, Mr. Niall MacBain,' but even as she finished the last word, he interrupted her. 'Wait, I should have said "Father," not guardian. And add "MacBain" after Garcia. André is my son.'

Strangely shocked, Alison said the only, absurd thing she could think of. 'I didn't know you were married.'

He looked at her, and a muscle moved and tightened in his dark jaw. 'Why should you know?' He turned and strode out of the schoolroom.

CHAPTER FOUR

ALISON found herself waiting for Wednesday to come, so that she might see this child, the son of Niall Mac-Bain. Clearly he had mentioned it to no one else in Shielbaig, for although news had filtered through in its usual magic way about the sale of Courthill, nothing was said about him being married with a child. He hadn't mentioned his wife, but that seemed, now, the logical reason for him buying Courthill. His father's cottage was very small, only two bedrooms, certainly not big enough for a suddenly expanded family. Alison was curious too about his wife. Would she be some exotic Brazilian beauty? She imagined that nothing but the best would do for Niall MacBain. If, too, she were rich, it would account for his apparent acquisition of a fortune. Yet, mused Alison, if indeed she were an heiress, would she be able to settle in such a quiet backwater as Shielbaig?

She set out from school towards home on Wednesday afternoon. She was in the car, because the day was heavily overcast. Niall's had been gone from the front of his father's house since the previous evening. Perhaps his wife and son had flown to Inverness the day before, from London, and he had gone to meet them, and spend a night there with them before beginning the last stage of their long journey. Perhaps he wanted to prepare them. Perhaps . . .

Alison shook herself mentally, and swung into the drive from the road. All this supposition, about a man who had upset her life so abruptly. He didn't matter. She must *make* him not matter, for if she was to live any sort of normal life in the future, it would be with him as a neighbour, and Alison knew that the strange mutual hatred could only destroy her, if she allowed it to. In an odd way, the fact of his being married might help, she thought.

She heard a car's engine, and through her rear view mirror, saw his car go past. Only for a moment, but it seemed as if he were alone.

By Thursday evening the news was all over the village. The different versions of the story were numerous, and would have been almost funny if Alison hadn't caught a glimpse of the child at the front room window when she passed on her way home from school Thursday lunchtime. He was small and pale, a little figure just standing holding on to the curtains as if for protection, wide-eyed, solemnly watching her as she walked past.

His face haunted Alison, and when she entered the post office after school that afternoon, a sudden silence fell, broken by Mrs. Finlayson who, quite unabashed, called out: 'Ach, 'tis only Alison. Tell us, is it true that Niall MacBain is married to a Brazilian coffee million-aire's daughter?'

Alison looked at her with genuine amazement on her face.

'I don't know, I don't imagine so,' she answered, very conscious that as the future teacher of his child, she should not indulge in gossip. 'I haven't seen his wife yet.'

'Nor have we,' chorused Daisy and Doris, the two

sisters who lived a couple of doors away from Fergus MacBain. They always wore pixie hoods, winter and summer, spent all their days at the front room window, and missed nothing that went on.

'But he arrived with this wee laddie yesterday, and the luggage—' said Daisy.

'—beautiful,' said Doris. 'All new, with big labels on—'

'—so we got out the glasses, and we could just read—'

'—as large as you like: "RIO–LONDRES." '

Conversation was difficult with them, for they constantly interrupted each other, but their meaning was clear. The little shop was so small that the two sisters, and another villager, Aggie Macdonald, and Alison, filled it, and they were all looking at her expectantly, as if she would know everything. The reason became obvious the next moment when Doris said: 'Did he not come to see you at school on Monday—'

'—saw him. So he was going to book the bairn in—'

'—and must have told you his name. Is it—'

There was another silence as Doris stopped in mid-sentence, not because of interruption, but because the door behind Alison was pushed gently, and Niall MacBain eased himself in. Doris and Daisy squeezed past, chorusing their greetings, which he returned quietly. Then Aggie murmured something about seeing to the tea, and Alison was left to order the groceries she had come to collect, very conscious of the big, silent man behind her.

She heard the rustle of paper, then the scratch of a pen, and Mrs. Finlayson pursed her lips and nodded, as if her worst suspicions had been confirmed. Alison wanted very much to escape from the shop, which had suddenly become too small for comfort. As she thanked the postmistress and turned to go out, she saw that he was filling in a telegram form. And she remembered the other one.

Outside in the fresh air, Alison took a deep breath. All this speculation was infectious. Because so little ever happened, anything that did was talked about and threshed over for weeks, even months. The villagers were getting plenty of tasty morsels to keep their appetites whetted, and Alison, who tried to keep a cool detachment about rumour and gossip, was finding herself enmeshed, equally fascinated, and wanting very much to know more about the mysterious boy, and the even more mysterious, as yet invisible wife.

Her mother and Jessie had each heard various versions of the rumours about Niall MacBain. He was divorced, he was widowed, his wife was coming next week, she was a Brazilian film star, an opera singer; the boy was unable to speak a word of English, he spoke it fluently . . . the stories were endless, all conjured up from the fertile minds of a few villagers with too little to do, and too much time to talk about others.

It was Jessie who spoke the first sensible words on the subject, of which Alison was rapidly tiring.

'And what,' she demanded, as they ate supper together in the kitchen, 'will the poor laddie do when school's over each day, and his father's working here? That wife of his had better turn up, or there will be one very lonely boy at that house. Can *you* see old man MacBain looking after him?' she demanded, looking at Alison and her mother. 'He'll be away on that bike of

his for his dram at the pub in Torrie, come what may,
And that's all he thinks about these days!'

The two of them looked at one another. Alison was
beginning to glimpse what would happen, and that
Jessie was right. And the question persisted. If Niall's
wife was coming, why hadn't she arrived at the same
time as her son?

Alison wondered if Niall would send the boy to school
alone on Monday morning. She hoped not, knowing
how overwhelming a strange place, and new faces,
could be to a young child.

As nine o'clock came, she looked at the seven shining, expectant faces, and she said: 'You all know we
have a new boy beginning today. He's a lot younger
than most of you, and he is from South America. I
hope you will all do your best to make him feel welcome.'

There was a murmured chorus of assent, above
which rose Fiona's clear voice.

'I've already met him,' she announced, looking
round. 'He's staying next door, and he's a shy wee
thing, so I'll help look after him, Miss.' As Alison was
about to thank her, Fiona added: 'He's cried himself to
sleep every night since he came.'

The words had the strangest effect on Alison. They
were like a hammer blow to the heart, hardly bearable.
She took a deep breath and said quietly: 'He's probably homesick, so we must make extra sure to be kind to
him.' But inside her heart cried out at the cruelty of an
insensitive father to let his child suffer so. How could
he? A little boy of six, scarcely more than a baby, to
have come, apparently alone from so far away to live in

a house with two men. No warm feminine arms to comfort him and soothe away the tears, just a cold bed in a small room, and perhaps not even a toy for company.

There was a small stirring of excitement in the class, and Alison looked up as the door opened, to see the little boy come in, his hand held firmly in Niall's. The picture they made at that moment so deeply etched itself into Alison's brain that she knew she would never be able to forget it as long as she lived. On the left the small pale-faced child, dressed in pullover, short trousers and jacket. Beside him, towering over everyone, filling the doorway, his father, looking towards Alison with no trace of the arrogant power in his features, but almost as if, for the first time, he were human.

She moved forward, her limbs acting mechanically, and as she reached them, held out her hand. 'Hello, André.' She waited, hoping desperately that he would respond. He did. His right hand came up into hers, and as she took it, she found herself looking into a pair of grey eyes so incredibly like his father's, yet with a strange defencelessness about them, that it caught her breath in her throat.

He was pale, his hair dark like Niall's, but soft and babyish, his nose small and straight, and no smile about his mouth, only the frightened look of a child who is trying very hard to be brave, but not quite succeeding.

Alison looked at Niall MacBain, and something of her feelings revealed themselves, for he gave a slight puzzled frown, then said:

'Is there anything you must ask me, Miss

Mackay?'

'No, Mr. MacBain. André will be all right here, don't worry. And I'll see him safely home at lunch time.'

'Thank you.' He turned to his son, detaching his hand gently, and touching the boy's head. ' 'Bye, André. Be good.' He was gone, moving silently across the room, and out, before Alison could speak, or think.

This first morning at school would be vitally important, she knew. The wrong impression now would adversely affect him for the rest of his schooldays. She looked around the class with a bright smile, grateful that she had a nice group of children. Rough though the boys undoubtedly were, they were kind-hearted, and living in such a small community there was a kinship about them that was heartening. Alison looked at Heather, at eight, the nearest in age to the new pupil. 'Heather, André will sit next to you – you may move your desk nearer. Fiona, come with me to the stockroom, and we'll fetch all the things André needs for his lessons.'

'Yes, Miss.' Both girls stood, Heather to go over to André and take his hand in a motherly way, Fiona to come to Alison's side.

As she saw the two children walk off to the desks at the side of the room, she felt lighter. She had done the right thing, she knew. Heather was a tall sturdy girl with a pretty face and a kind heart. Between her and Fiona there would be friendly rivalry as to who could look after the new arrival best. And both, in their own ways, were adept at lavishing scorn on any boy who might be tempted to bully their protégé.

The morning went well. Alison avoided fussing

André, preferring to let him find his feet with the children in his own way. She soon discovered that he was bright and intelligent, spoke English with a quaint accent, but sufficiently well to make himself understood by the others.

At playtime she remained behind in the classroom and watched curiously to see how this small edition of Niall MacBain would mix with the rough older boys, but he wisely decided to play safe, and remained with the two girls. Alison turned away, smiling. He was doing well enough for his first morning.

And so his life at Shielbaig school began. A turning point for him, and although she did not know it, for Alison too.

She did not see anything of Niall for several days after that. His car was always outside his father's house at lunch and home time, and André seemed, as each day passed, to be settling in better, and even began to smile when the others spoke to him and showed him their playground games. Alison was aware that he was painfully shy, deeply aware too that there was nothing she could do to help, except to try and protect him from the unconscious cruelty of children when they might try and ask him questions about where he had come from.

She said good-bye to him on Friday with a heavy heart, praying inwardly that Niall would let him play out with the other children at the loch side over the weekend. He looked as if he needed fresh air and good food to build him up, and Alison knew, from casual remarks passed by the other children, that once home from school each day, he was not seen out of doors until the following morning.

She told Jessie about this when they sat in the kitchen drinking tea after she reached home that day. Jessie was busy making crowdie, the soft white cheese they loved to eat on jam-covered oatcakes at weekends. The old housekeeper looked up from her vigorous beating with the wooden spoon in the basin, and her eyes appraised Alison shrewdly.

'Ach, you've taken to that bairn, haven't you?'

'I – yes, I have,' Alison admitted, warmly aware that little escaped Jessie's eye.

'Hmph! Considering your feelings for his father, I call that rather strange!' she said.

'My feelings towards Niall MacBain have nothing to do with it,' Alison answered. 'You'd know why, if you met him. He's a poor wee scrap of humanity, dragged half way across the world on his own, and wanting nothing so much as a woman to cuddle him.' She bit her lip, aware that she was giving herself away.

Jessie sighed. 'Ach, Alison, I'm sorry. If you could see your face, child! There's only one thing for it, that I can see. You must, for the boy's sake, tackle MacBain when he comes again. Ask him when his wife is coming – and tell him why.'

Alison looked up from her tea, aghast. 'Jessie, I couldn't do that! I can barely talk to him without – why, he'd jump on me like – oh, no!' She shuddered.

'For the wee child's sake,' Jessie looked at Alison, and there came something in Jessie's eyes that struck an instant response in hers, and they understood one another perfectly. Jessie, peaceable and good-humoured, would, if she saw any injustice, turn into a raging tigress. And in that moment of mutual comprehension, Alison saw the spark that told her what Jessie said was right and just. She stood up slowly, and she smiled. 'Yes, Jessie, I will,' she said.

Jessie smiled back. 'Aye, that you will,' she answered. 'And it can be tonight, for he's coming round.'

'Why, you—' Alison began to laugh. 'You crafty old woman!'

'Me?' Eyes wide with innocence, the housekeeper looked round, as if Alison must be talking to someone else.

Then it sank in. 'Why is he coming?' she asked.

Jessie shrugged. 'Just a few details to sort out, I suppose. The building materials will be arriving next week, and then the work will be starting, once everything is signed.'

'First we'll have to move out,' Alison said very quietly.

'Aye, that we will. But there is someone coming to decorate the cottage next week, before we go in.'

'What?' Alison whirled round. 'When was that decided?'

'Ach, I don't know. They talked it over. Your mother is no doubt wanting to surprise you – so don't let on I've told you, for heaven's sake.'

'No, I won't. Don't worry, Jessie.' But she felt strangely hurt that all this should be going on without her knowing. It was almost as if her mother was in conspiracy with Niall MacBain, and Alison was gradually being shut out. It was probably her imagination, she knew, but already there seemed a difference in her mother. She walked and talked with new purpose in her, as if she were coming to life again, and Alison

75

knew that it was because of the work she would be doing for him.

When Niall MacBain arrived, Alison was sitting in the lounge with her mother, watching television. They heard the ring at the door, and she jumped up. 'I'll let him in. I want a word with him.'

'Alison—' her mother began. Alison looked at her. 'It's all right. It's about his son.'

She opened the door to see him standing there, larger than life and very formidable; she quaked inwardly. He would not tolerate interference. Then, as she remembered André's wistful face at the window, Alison found her voice. 'Mr. MacBain, before I take you in to my mother, may I have a word with you?'

He came into the hall, his grey eyes on her, and narrowing slightly at her words. 'Yes, what is it?'

'It's about your son,' she began. She wished they were anywhere but in the hall. It was so vast. A smaller room would have been less overpowering, but she had begun, and she had to go on before her courage evaporated in the face of his overwhelming hostility.

'You'll think I'm interfering, and for that I beg your indulgence, for I'm thinking only of André.' As she spoke, she regained her composure, and met his cold glance with the clear gaze of complete frankness. 'It's this. He's only young, and so helpless. I wonder if I might ask when your wife will be coming? And also – will you please let him play out with the other children after school?'

His face had gradually darkened as she had been talking, and when she stopped there was an awful silence. When it was stretched to breaking point, he said softly: 'Is that all?'

Alison swallowed. 'Yes.'

'Then I'll take your second question first. André is a delicate boy, not used to playing games. He has been a sickly child, and is only just now getting stronger. When he's more used to school, yes, I will let him play out, for I realize, as you do, the value of fresh air. As to your other question, what reason have you for asking it?'

'If *you* have to ask that,' she burst out, 'you wouldn't understand when I told you.'

'Try me,' he suggested, steely hard.

She took a deep breath. 'All right, I will. I'm speaking as his teacher now, so this has nothing personal in it at all. Do you understand?'

'I think so,' and those grey eyes never left her face for a moment.

'He – he needs a woman's love, someone to be there, to comfort him when he's homesick, or lonely, as he undoubtedly is at times, in such a completely different country. He's little more than a baby to be without his mother, and I—' she paused, blinking back the treacherous tears as she went on: 'I heard from a pupil who lives next door to you that he had cried himself to sleep the first few nights – and it was like a pain in my heart to hear it, Mr. MacBain. Oh, I know it sounds awfully stupid and sentimental, and men like their sons to grow up tough, but please, he's such a lovely little boy, I can't keep silent any longer.' She closed her eyes.

'I believe you care.'

'Yes, I do, very much.' She could meet his gaze again, in a strange kind of temporary truce. And she saw his lowered glance, as if he was unsure of himself,

77

then he looked up. 'Then I'll tell you. His mother won't be coming. She's dead. She died a short time ago, in Rio de Janeiro. All he has now is me.'

The words sank in slowly. As their full impact struck her, Alison gasped: 'Oh, no! I'm so terribly sorry – I didn't know.'

'How could you? I've only told you now because I believe you are genuinely interested in the boy's welfare. For that I thank you. But you see, there's nothing I can do. He's going to have to grow up the hard way, as I did.'

Alison shook her head. 'Please forgive me for asking. I'll take you in to my mother.' Just before he reached the door, a thought struck her. 'What's going to happen when you're working on the house? Who will look after him then?'

He stopped. 'I hadn't looked that far ahead. My main concern was to get him here before—' he paused, then went on: 'I'll think of something. My father is at home, and there will be other men working here as well as me. I don't have to be here all the time.'

'I see.' But as she opened the door, she wondered what he had been about to say. 'Here's Mr. MacBain, Mother.'

'Thank you.' He stepped past her, and went in, and she moved away. So André was truly alone. Poor child, no wonder he looked so sad and lost. Her arms ached to comfort that tiny frail body.

The building materials began to arrive the following week. A lorry was parked by the garage when Alison went home on the Monday afternoon, and two men were unloading wood, and sacks of plaster. She recog-

78

nized them as two brothers from Strathcorran and greeted them, wondering if they would be coming to do the work. Shy and hardworking, Alison knew them to be good craftsmen. Niall MacBain, it seemed, knew what he was about.

Jessie greeted her with the words:

'Your mother's at the cottage. She said will you go as soon as you come in.'

Alison put her bag down on the rocker. 'I'll away now, Jessie.'

She wasn't prepared for what she would see when she reached the cottage, an L-shaped bungalow. The door was open, and she could hear voices, and assumed that Niall was there with her mother. But it wasn't he who stood in the main living-room with Mrs. Mackay. It was someone she remembered very well from a fateful dance, now a man, and good-looking in a very different way – Johnny Gordon.

Hiding her astonishment as best she could, Alison went forward. He turned and smiled, then held out his hand.

'Hello, Alison,' he said, in his slow quiet voice.

They shook hands, and all she could think of, in that moment of utter astonishment, was: surely this man isn't the wolf that Niall MacBain fought, after that memorable dance? It seemed incredible. Gone was the brash, hot-eyed boy. In his place was a tall, well set up man of about thirty, dressed simply in jeans and dark fisherman's jersey. Sandy-haired, blue-eyed, his skin was tanned and healthy. She smiled back. 'Hello, Johnny.'

'Johnny is coming to decorate for us here,' her mother said. 'I thought we might talk it over at the house. He can get the paper and paint from Inverness tomorrow.'

'Aye, and then I'll begin at Courthill next week, with the Cameron brothers. Well, I think I have all the measurements I need.' He tapped an old notebook in his hand. 'If you would look through the pattern books I have left at the big house, you can decide.'

'You'll stay and have some tea?' Mrs. Mackay asked.

He smiled. 'That's very kind of you.'

He looked across at Alison, and she saw a spark of something that made her go warm. Her mother said: 'We'll away now. You know, I'm thinking this old place won't look so bad at all when it's done up.'

They walked slowly back, and Alison wondered at Niall MacBain's choice. She knew that Johnny Gordon had his own small business near Strathcorran. He did general building work and repairs, and, presumably, decorating as well. Niall couldn't have known this, for he had been away for nine years. Alison didn't imagine old Fergus was fond of letter writing, which left her with one conclusion. All this had been in Niall MacBain's mind for a while, and perhaps he had asked John Stewart, the solicitor, to look around for him. It was almost frightening, as though there were an inevitability about everything. Things were happening so swiftly, too, that Alison began to feel as if everything was slipping past her rapidly, and already, at night, when she went to bed, her head was a whirl of thoughts, and ideas, and fears, so that she could scarcely sleep. One thing above all disturbed her. More than the fact of losing her home – she was becoming reconciled to that – or her mother's deciding to work for the 'enemy', more even than the feud itself, and the mutual dislike between her and Niall, overriding all this, one fact was constant. The small, wistful face of Niall's son haunted and disturbed her. She wanted so very much to help him. She could do it only during those few precious hours he was in her charge, and she made the most of them. Gradually, as the days had passed, she sensed a response from him, an opening of spirit, like a flower to the light. She wanted so desperately to succeed, to see him a normal happy boy, and she knew she must, for her own peace of mind.

Something was to happen that following week to help Alison in her personal task, though she did not know it.

On Wednesday, Niall took André to school after lunch. Alison had gone back a few minutes early, and was alone in the class, looking through various drawings from the past term's art lessons. She looked up as the door opened, and the two walked in. She stood up and went towards them, and as she did so, a strange thing happened. André pulled away from Niall and came to her with a smile.

'Hello, André.' She took his hand, then looked up, surprising a rather odd expression on Niall's face. 'Yes, Mr. MacBain, is there something wrong?'

It was strange, but at the times when André was with him, they seemed to have an unspoken truce, almost as if they both knew that it was important to tread carefully.

He shook his head, and a slight smile lifted the corners of his mouth. 'No, but I have a favour to ask. Would you be good enough to take André home with you at four o'clock? I have to go to the solicitor with your mother. I went to see her this morning, and Jessie told me that she will look after him until we get back to Courthill.'

Something made her answer more hotly than she intended. 'I would be prepared to look after him.'

There was a small silence. Then he said: 'I'm sorry, I didn't mean it that way. I imagined you'd be busy after school.'

His apology shook her. She hadn't thought him capable of anything so human, nor had she intended answering him so sharply, but she had been stung by the implication that she wouldn't want to have André outside school hours.

'I usually am. But I'm quite sure André won't be any trouble.' She ruffled the boy's hair. 'Will you like that, coming home with me, and meeting my dog?'

He looked up, smiled, but said nothing. He had the disconcerting habit of occasionally not answering questions, but giving a smile instead. Alison had already decided he understood quite well, but just didn't feel like making the effort to speak, and for the moment, she wasn't prepared to correct him. They were learning gradually to get on, she and André, and to understand one another.

'Then that's settled.' She looked at his father. 'He'll be well cared for until you return. Jessie will give him some tea, if you'd like. We generally have a light meal at four-thirty.'

'Thank you.' He turned to his son. 'You hear, André? Be good. I'll come for you at Miss Mackay's. Good-bye.'

After he had gone, Alison said: 'That will be fun, won't it?'

He thought about that for a moment. She had also discovered that he took every question very seriously, and weighed it carefully before he decided to answer. Now, after a few seconds' thoughtful silence, he said: 'I do not know if I like dogs.'

'Oh, I see!' She was relieved. 'Well, I'm sure you'll like Rusty. She's a nice old lady dog, and very kind to little boys.'

He gave that remark some frowning consideration, then nodded, and without another word, trotted to his desk and sat down.

The arrival of the other children was heralded by scuffling and muffled laughter as one of them fell outside, then the door burst open, and the afternoon began.

'We have a rocking horse in the attic. Would you like to see it?' Alison was showing André round the house. At her question he looked up and smiled. She took this for assent, and they began the steep climb up the attic stairs.

She watched his face at the first sight of the huge dappled horse, the brown leather saddle well worn but still showing faint traces of a shine, his eyes as bright as ever, even after years in the dusty attic.

'May I touch her?' André asked, after studying the horse for a few moments.

'Of course. His name is Pegasus.' As he made a careful way over the jumble of years, she added: 'You may ride him if you like.'

André stood beside Pegasus; for a moment he was still, then he reached out his hand and carefully, very gently, he stroked the rough hair mane that had so fascinated Alison as a child. The horse rocked very slightly, a mere stirring at his touch, and he turned a startled face to her.

'It's all right.' She crossed quickly to his side, and pushed the large wooden creature. 'See – he goes up and down. Watch.'

She climbed on, held the reins, and rocked to and fro as she said: 'Whoa, Peg, old boy!' She looked to see the boy laughing delightedly, his small white teeth like little pearls.

'Oh, she – he is good. He is good. I like.'

Alison slid off his back. 'Then try. I'll hold you.'

Gently she lifted him on, a gossamer weight in her arms, put the reins in his hands, and holding him securely, started to rock the horse gently. After the first startled moment when he clutched at her in fright, she felt his small body relax, and eased her hand slightly away. He was chuckling with pleasure, making clicking sounds with his teeth, oblivious of her, of everything except the horse. This was a different child altogether from the one she had seen looking out of the window of his grandfather's house. And she knew that Pegasus should belong to him. It would be fitting in a way, for the horse would then remain in the house he had lived in for over fifty years.

Something, perhaps a slight sound, made her turn, and she started as she saw the movement in the shadows of the doorway. Niall MacBain was watching them. He came in then.

'I didn't mean to make you jump,' he said. 'I was watching André riding the horse.'

'Have you been here long?' She felt slightly confused, as if he had eavesdropped on her thoughts.

'A minute or two, that's all. I didn't like to disturb you.'

Alison had to take a deep breath to curb the odd breathlessness that had begun. She looked at her watch. 'We'd better go down now, Jessie was making some sandwiches for André.'

'Yes. She sent me up to fetch you.' His eyes were very still upon her; very level. She turned and lifted André from the horse. 'There now. Did you like that?'

He looked up at her, eyes shining. 'I like her very much.'

'If your father will allow you to have Pegasus, he's yours.' Alison looked at the man as she said it, realizing that she should have perhaps left it until André wasn't there, in case . . .

'Are you sure? It must have been in the family for years—'

'Quite sure,' she answered. 'We'll have no room at the cottage. I would truly like André to have it.' She looked down at the little boy, and was startled to see tears well up in his eyes. Then suddenly he put his arms up to her, and she bent instinctively to feel them slide round her neck. As she straightened, she lifted him with her. He was so small, but his arms were strong as he squeezed them round her neck, and whispered fiercely: 'You are a good lady. I would like very much—' then he stopped, as if remembering his father was there. '*Papa*, may I, please?'

'Yes, André, you may. Say thank you to Miss Mackay.'

'I thank you, Mees Mackay.'

'You're very welcome.' She began to walk to the

door, still carrying him. She trod very carefully over the piles of books and magazines, but André obscured her view, and as she put her foot down hard on a book, it moved slightly with the weight, so that she lost her balance. Niall moved in that instant of time before she fell. One hand to André, steadying him, the other round Alison's waist. It was only for a moment. She regained her balance, he lifted André from her and put him on his feet at the door, with the words: 'Down you go.'

Alison couldn't have put it into words, nor would she have wanted to, but something changed in that moment. The atmosphere was charged with a tension so brittle that it seemed the air crackled with it. She said breathlessly: 'Thank you,' and went past him as he stood back in the doorway. She had never been so sharply aware of another person's nearness before, so strongly conscious of the masculinity of the tall powerful figure standing so still beside her. Then she was going down the stairs with André, and it was as if nothing had happened. It had been her imagination, of course. She was tired, she had not been sleeping well lately, not since knowing they were moving, and that, and the worry of the school . . . But she knew it wasn't only those things. She had, in that moment of startled awareness, been conscious of an overwhelming desire to have Niall go on holding her. Absurd, of course! How Meg would laugh when she told her, Alison thought. She would put it all into perspective. The poor frustrated teacher who swoons when the parent of a pupil touches her! Alison could imagine her witty interpretation of the situation, and smiled reluctantly to herself. It was funny, really funny – for they didn't even like one another.

It was all settled. The house – her home – was no longer theirs. It belonged legally to Niall MacBain. Johnny Gordon was working in the cottage, wall-papering, painting, and repairing, and the wood and plaster and all the other things needed for the alteration of Courthill into a hotel were stored in the garages at the back of the house. There was so much work to be done, but it would be completed, and then the strangers would come, and perhaps part of her would die. It would take months before that happened, and during the time she would have to learn to live with the fact. Alison blessed the day she had decided to become a teacher. There was such infinite variety and hard work in teaching even a small number of children that she had less time to brood about Courthill. And there was André. Every day he was creeping further into her heart, and every day she watched him become a little stronger, a shade less dependent on others, and she had to stop herself feeling proud. It was not her doing, it was his own. He was a clever, sensitive child, and knew immediately what was wanted of him. She liked him so much, yet she had to hide her feelings, had to remind herself whose son he was.

Her mother was rarely seen. She was so busy in her studio, drawing, designing the layout for the hotel that Alison scarcely saw anything of her. She admitted, reluctantly, to Jessie that it was a change to see her mother so purposeful. She had seen some of the drawings, and they were very good. The hall had been transformed, on paper, into a modern reception area that would do justice to any hotel anywhere in the world. As she looked at the drawings, Alison could see the love and skill that her mother was putting into her work. A stranger could not have done nearly so well, however clever.

Jessie agreed with her. It was after school two days later, Friday. They were in the kitchen, Alison with her cup of tea, Jessie busily sorting out drawers, ready for the move the following week. Alison looked round the enormous room and sighed. 'Oh, Jessie, he'll have gleaming new cookers here soon, and a new sink unit. It won't be the same place.'

'That it won't,' Jessie agreed. 'Ach, and I would not mind doing the cooking for him!'

'Jessie!'

The old woman began to chuckle at Alison's gasp.

'Well, your mother is already working for him. My guess is he'll find something else for her to do when the place is completed – after all, there is always a lot to do in any hotel.'

'But you – you'd work for him, here?'

'Aye,' Jessie pursed her lips. 'Only on a part-time basis, of course. I wouldn't ever leave you or your mother, for we are like a family. But he'd be fine to work for, fair and just.'

'How do you know?' Alison asked derisively.

Jessie nodded. 'I know! I'm old enough to weigh people up. Yon Niall MacBain is a bonny man right enough. Make no mistake about it.'

'You surprise me.' Alison looked at her in amazement.

'Aye, well, maybe I do. But it's the truth. And can you not see yourself what he's like?'

Alison pretended to shudder. 'Yes, I can. The less I

have to do with him, the better.'

'And his son?' asked Jessie softly.

'That's not fair!' Alison protested. 'He's a child. As far as I can see he's not a bit like his father, except in looks. He's certainly not like *he* was as a boy, thank the lord!'

Jessie looked at Alison shrewdly, then gave a little smile. 'That's a fact.' Suddenly realizing that she was wasting time, she began pulling out drawers. 'This won't get the place empty, will it?'

Alison stood up. 'No. And I'd better go and do the same in my bedroom. Oh, Jessie, do you think we'll be happy in the cottage?'

'Of course we will.' Jessie laughed. 'It'll be warmer, and cosier – we won't know ourselves in winter.'

Alison smiled. 'I hope you're right. And there'll be no guests at Courthill in winter – come to that, I can't imagine so many in summer either, yet he seems to know what he's doing—' and as she said the words, an odd expression flitted across Jessie's face, and was gone. Alison stopped, some instinct forcing her to say: 'Jessie, what is it?'

The housekeeper shook her head. 'Nothing – nothing much.'

'Yes, there is. Just now, when I was saying about guests, you looked almost as if you knew something.'

'Aye, well, it was just that I was hearin' a wee rumour, that's all.' And she turned away, busying herself rummaging in the old knife drawer.

'A rumour about what?' Alison persisted.

Jessie looked at her. 'I will not tell you, for it may not be true, and I'm the last one to want to cause trouble.

I'm sorry, Alison, but there it is.'

And she would not say another word.

The following day Alison found out for herself what Jessie meant. It happened in the shop, where she had gone to buy vegetables and tinned food for Jessie, and while Mrs. Finlayson was serving her, another woman walked in. Alison recognized her as a niece of Doris and Daisy, named Alice. She lived in Strathcorran and called regularly to visit her aunts. She was a small woman with birdlike eyes that constantly darted about in a disconcerting manner, as if she might miss something. She greeted Alison with: 'Well, it's the teacher, is it?'

Alison agreed that it was, and said hello as pleasantly as possible. Alice was nosier than her aunts, and not so harmless.

'Ach well, 'tis a shame you have to leave the big house after all these years, and a hotel, is it, that it will be?'

'Yes,' Alison said shortly. 'Mrs. Finlayson, did I ask you for sugar?'

'Aye, he knows what he's about, that young fellow, does he not? I said to my aunts just now, I said: "He'll go far, that one." There'll be good money made with the new road opening, and the skiing too. Fancy it! This old place will be like Aviemore in a few years.'

Alison had to put her hand on the counter to prevent herself from falling. The shock was so intense that she felt herself go white, and heard Mrs. Finlayson's voice, as if from a great distance, saying: 'Why, what is it? Shall I bring you a glass of water?'

'Please.' Her lips felt dry. She took the glass and drank thirstily. At all costs she knew she must not show her feelings to these women. It would be all over the village in five minutes. She managed to smile. 'Thank you. I had a sudden dizzy spell. I must be anaemic.' She looked at Alice, and said lightly: 'You were saying about the new road. Yes, it certainly will make a big difference here. I didn't think many people knew about it.'

Alice smiled smugly. 'Aye, well, it's supposed to be a secret, but my brother works for the Council, so *he* gets to know these things.'

Mrs. Finlayson decided she had been silent long enough. 'Aye, and young MacBain would know, for doesn't his uncle work in the Highway Department in Inverness, and you can be sure he'd pass on a bit of news like that.' She smiled at Alison. 'You maybe should have held on a wee bit longer. There would have been more interest in Courthill with it being right in the centre of everything. Aye, we'll be busy here soon enough.'

Alison managed to escape eventually. In the safety and coolness of the woods on the way home, she stopped and put down her basket. She was trembling with a mixture of shock and rage. Shock at hearing news so startling, yet having to hide her natural reaction, and rage with the man who had coolly bought their house from them, knowing that he was practically stealing it, because with a new road, and a ski resort planned, its value would at the very least double within weeks of the news getting out.

Oh yes, he had been clever all right, very clever, she thought bitterly. How he must have laughed all the time he was ushering her mother to the solicitors, and asking her to design the layout. That was to keep her quiet and happy. And Jessie had heard, and knowing she could do nothing, had kept quiet. Alison felt almost ill at his treachery. He had certainly had his revenge with a bonus.

Just days ago, when she had been with André in the attic, she had sensed a difference about him, seen another side to his nature. How wrong I've been, she thought. He hasn't changed at all! The years had made him more cunning, that was all. She bent to pick up the basket, and heard his voice say: 'I'll take that.' And Alison whirled round to see Niall walking towards her.

CHAPTER FIVE

ALISON waited for him to reach her, and she watched him, the loathing she felt filling her eyes, and spilling out in tears.

He stopped, and frowned. 'What's the matter?' And as he spoke he held out a hand to take the basket. She moved it away, and saw his face change. Eyes narrowed, he spoke softly. 'All right. You look as if you want to hit me. Out with it.' His grey eyes met Alison's challengingly, and she knew that this was the moment of truth.

'I've just now heard that there'll be a road coming by here, a major road from the south – a new direct one that will bring lots of people to the new ski resort that's planned.'

'Well?' His voice was level.

'Did you know about it?' Alison tried to keep her voice even, but with the greatest difficulty. Then she saw him smile slightly, and clenched her hands on the basket handle to keep control.

'So that's it!' He spoke softly, as if to himself.

'Did you know?' she repeated, her voice rising slightly.

He looked down at her, his eyes very steady on hers. 'Maybe.'

'Then you stole Courthill from us! You knew, and you let my mother sell it to you at a low price because—' Alison's voice broke, and she felt stifled. 'You're no better than a thief!'

She saw the muscles tighten in his cheek, saw the flare of anger in his eyes, to match her own. But he kept his voice still low as he answered her. 'I should choose my words more carefully if I were you.'

'Why? There are no witnesses to hear us,' she spat back. 'I shall say what I like to you. You're a cheat! You gambled on my mother's not knowing about the road, and won. She didn't know, so you got the house cheap. Are you proud of yourself?'

'So you think that's what happened? Everything is so clear-cut to you, isn't it? Either black or white, no shades in between. I bought the house, I knew about the road, therefore I'm a thief and a cheat. You haven't called me a liar yet. Did you forget that one?'

She spun round, to move away, and his hand shot out and closed over hers, making her drop the basket, which fell to the ground and toppled on its side. He pulled her slightly towards him.

'Don't walk away when I'm talking to you. You started it, remember? Never walk away in the middle of a fight, or you'll lose.'

'Let me go!' Furiously she tried to pull her arm free, but his grip was as steel. 'You're too despicable to speak to!' Her chest heaved with the effort to breathe, and she felt weak. 'There's nothing more to be said. The house is yours now, so you've won.'

'But I haven't finished with *you* yet,' he said. 'You seem to think you can make wild accusations about me any time you like with impunity, just because you're Alison Mackay. Get that out of your head right now. I will not be called a thief by you or anyone. Just for the record, I don't tell lies either. I didn't when I was a boy, and I don't intend to start now. I bought your house at a fair price, and if you don't believe me, you can ask your mother.'

Something in his tone made her pause in her efforts to free herself. He hadn't denied knowledge of the road, but some assurance in his voice puzzled her. There was no guilt on his face, as there should have been. And then Alison remembered something that she had known subconsciously all along. A faint memory dredged from the mists of the past; childish words said in anger after a fight between Alec and Niall, witnessed by her. Words soon forgotten – except by her.

'You said just now that you never told lies,' she managed to get out. 'Then something you said years ago, when you were about eleven, must also have been true.'

'What did I say?' He had not once raised his voice, and it was somehow more frightening than if he had shouted. Yet she had to go on, had to know the truth, at whatever cost to herself and her peace of mind. Running her tongue over suddenly dry lips, she said: 'You told Alec after a fight that Courthill was really yours – that you and your family should be living there instead of us–' she winced, then gasped as his hand tightened on her wrist, and suddenly she was frightened. 'Let go of me!'

Abruptly he did so, and she saw the expression, almost of pain on his face. It was gone in an instant, and his eyes hardened as he looked down at her. 'You have an even better memory than I thought.'

'What did you mean by it?'

He shrugged. 'It doesn't matter now.'

'Yes, it does. If – as you say – you never tell lies, then

that must have been the truth as you knew it. So what did you mean?'

'I said forget it. It doesn't matter now, because Courthill is mine.' For the first time his voice reflected his anger, no longer quiet, but harsher. For some reason she had touched him on the raw. And because she still wanted to hurt him, she said: 'Then I must draw my own conclusions. I can only assume that we stole Courthill from the MacBains at some time in the past. Perhaps before the feud? Is that it? Tell me – is it? Her voice had a ragged edge to it, as if she had been running, and the odd breathlessness was back. There was something far deeper than she had suspected here, she knew, and as he turned away, it was her turn to stop him. She reached out and gripped his arm with all her strength. 'Answer me!' she cried. She felt the hard muscles under her hand as he turned, and she gasped at the expression on his face. She saw it only for a second, as the next moment everything was blotted out as he bent and kissed her with brutal hardness. She was too stunned to move, then realized what was happening, and pushed him away.

'How dare you do that!' she gasped. This had happened before, in nearly the same spot, nine years ago – but what a difference! Then his mouth had been boyish, the kiss clumsy and breathless. Now, a hardness, a taste of the experience that had gone into the years between, left her feeling weak and confused.

'That's all the answer you'll get from me,' he said. 'And what have you got to say to that?' His voice had lost its quietness; he spoke more quickly, and Alison suddenly realized that the kiss had had more of an effect on him than he had intended. His eyes were darker, shadowed, and as he stood watching her, the air seemed to crackle with electric tension. It was all around them in that cool green light, the trees silent witnesses to a kiss that had obviously been as much a surprise to him as it had to her.

'If that's the way you deal with questions you don't like,' she said shakily, trying to dispel the tension, which was making her terribly uneasy, 'it must make life very difficult for you. Don't ever do it again,' she took a deep breath, 'or you'll be sorry.'

'Threats?' he asked, and a muscle twitched at the corner of his mouth. 'I react differently to threats from most people. To me they're a challenge – you might do well to remember that, Miss Mackay.' His eyes flickered down to the basket which still lay on the ground. He bent and picked it up, then handed it to her. 'I don't offer my help twice, either.' And he strode off towards Courthill, leaving Alison standing there. Her heart thudded rapidly, and she was more confused than ever before. She had the obscure feeling that she had just lost an argument.

And so the work began at Courthill. They planned to move the following Wednesday, the day after Johnny finished decorating. He had done a good job, inside and out, and the white walls gleamed in the afternoon sun as Alison walked to it on Tuesday after school. The front door was open, and she went into the small hall. The smell of paint still lingered in the air, even though Johnny had left all the windows open. The large living-room was to her left. This, with pine walls and ceiling, had been left as it was, the beauty of the wood brought out only by Johnny's skilful polishing. The kitchen, on the other side of the living-room, gleamed warm honey gold, and through the window was a breathtaking view of the loch. The cottage was L-shaped, and Alison had the same view from her bedroom window. She smiled to herself, wondering what Rusty would make of the move. She decided to move the dog's basket into her room for the first few nights.

'Anyone here?' It was a man's voice, and she stiffened, fearing Niall MacBain. She hadn't seen him since Saturday, she didn't want to see him, and the fact that he had paid to have their new home decorated only added fuel to her burning resentment. Her mother was so pleased, and had expected Alison to be equally impressed. She can't see his motives as I can, she thought. Even when Alison had tackled her mother on the Saturday evening about the new road, Mrs. Mackay had insisted that all Niall's actions had been fair and above board. The road wasn't definite, it was all very much a gamble whether it was ever built, and everyone knew they took years to actually *do* anything – he had hypnotized her well. Alison gave up in the end and went to bed, seething with suppressed anger.

Now she turned and saw with relief that her caller was Johnny Gordon.

'I was admiring your work,' she told him. 'You've done a wonderful job. Especially here.' She waved her arm round at the kitchen, the smart white cupboards, gleaming sink, everything just so, for them to move in. He grinned and looked at her, and what she saw in his eyes made her suddenly warm. She knew that gleam of masculine admiration when she saw it – and something more – but she was no longer a foolish teenager, and it didn't bother her. He spoke quietly enough, never taking his eyes off her.

'Aye, it's not bad,' he admitted, and Alison wondered why she had thought he had changed, the other day. It was still there all right, but more subdued – perhaps more dangerous. She might have to watch Johnny Gordon, she decided. He was no longer a boy.

'You're moving in tomorrow, Alison?'

'Yes. If I could get the day from school I would, but it's impossible. There's no relief teacher for miles.'

'Well, the Cameron boys will be here, and me. We'll be bringing everything across for your mother. And the furniture that's staying at the big house for when it's a hotel will be stacked in one of the bedrooms that's having no alterations done.'

Alison bit her lip. When her mother had told her that Niall wanted to buy their surplus furniture, she had had mixed feelings. It seemed on the face of it an ideal solution, for seeing it go to be sold in an auction would have been heartbreaking. It was old and solid and good, and wouldn't fetch anything like its value. Now, that wouldn't happen. Yet it seemed as if he were taking more and more all the time, taking everything she knew and loved for his own.

'So I might come home from school to find the work all done,' she said lightly, forcing a smile. He wasn't so easily fooled as she thought, for he gave her a shrewd look.

'Aye, that's true. It will be a wrench for you, living here I mean, instead of Courthill.'

'We'll get used to it.' She opened a cupboard door. 'Jessie will find it easier, I imagine. The other kitchen is enormous.'

99

He nodded. 'That it is. Well—' he looked at his watch, 'I'll best away. It will be an early start in the morning. The sooner everything is moved out, the sooner we can begin the work there.'

'Johnny,' she said, and he turned slowly. 'How did Niall MacBain come to ask you to work for him?'

'Mr. Stewart arranged for all of us. Did you not know?'

'I know very little of his plans,' she answered, and there was a trace of bitterness in her tone. She saw him glance sharply at her before saying: 'So it's like that, is it?'

'Like what?'

He shrugged. 'Och, word gets around. The feud's never been forgotten hereabouts. People have long memories, you know.'

'I've lived here all my life, Johnny. I know.'

'They say he's changed. They say he goes all out to get just what he wants.'

Alison shivered. So it wasn't only her. 'And what do you think?'

Again the shrug. 'I think they're right. But he's a good man to work for, I'll say that. There's no nonsense with him. He tells you what he wants doing – and he expects it to be done.' He paused, then added: 'He's paying me well. He'll get a good job done by all of us.'

'I'm sure he will.' Alison began to walk to the door. 'Will you come home for a cup of tea before you go?'

He grinned suddenly. 'I was hoping you'd ask.'

They began to walk back to the house, Johnny beside her as they went through the tall thick trees. So lost was she in thought about the move that she didn't look where she was going, and a jutting out twig caught in her hair as she passed it, jerking her to a standstill as she gave an exclamation of surprise.

Johnny stopped, turned, then saw her predicament. 'Stay still,' he ordered, and pulled the offending twig free. 'You should look where you're going,' he told her, amused, and put his hand to her hair. 'Mind now, you're all bits of twigs and leaves – you'll be full of tangles tonight when you comb your hair.'

But he seemed to be taking his time, and Alison moved away with a laugh. 'I'll manage,' she said. For she guessed what was in his mind, and she had already had enough trouble in the woods; she wanted no more.

He caught up with her and touched her arm lightly. 'Did you think I was going to kiss you?' he asked, in a curious voice.

'Not at all!' Alison tried to sound astonished, but kept on walking.

He began to laugh. 'Well, I was. So don't say you've not been warned. I may try again.'

'Will you now? Thank you for telling me.' As they came in sight of the house, she added: 'I shall have to keep out of your way, won't I?'

'Will you?' He gave her a slanting sideways look. 'No, don't do that, please, Alison. You're one of the reasons that I took the job.'

'Oh, really, Johnny!' she burst out in amused disbelief.

'It's true! I wanted to see what you were like, after all these years. Och, I've seen you, yes. But only from a distance, never to speak to. And I'll never forget that night of the dance—'

'No!' she whirled round on him. 'Don't mention that. It's one night I want to forget.'

He backed a few inches, pretending alarm. 'Hey, I'm sorry—' His eyes became wary. 'What did he do?'

'Niall MacBain? Nothing! Why do you ask like that?'

He grinned reminiscently, and stroked his jaw. 'Because I followed you, hoping for a kiss – and got a punch on the chin for my pains. Perhaps I have a right to ask.'

Alison tried vainly to keep her face straight. 'I'm sorry, Johnny, but it was your own fault.' Laughter bubbled through. 'He – he'd only come to poach trout!'

'That's not what he said to me.'

Suddenly sobered by something in his voice, Alison stopped laughing. 'Why, what did he say?' she asked quietly.

He looked at her almost regretfully. 'Och, it doesna' matter. It's too long ago—'

'Then tell me – please.'

'He said: "She's mine, boy, not yours – mine." And I shall not forget the look on his face when he said it, ever.'

Those strange words of Johnny's and the way he'd said them came back to Alison the following night. It was late, and both her mother and Jessie had gone to bed exhausted after the move. She looked around her new bedroom, and Rusty, from her basket in the corner, looked up and thumped her tail sadly as if in sympathy. Alison swallowed hard, wondering if she would ever sleep. The room was so much smaller than her old one. Brightly decorated, with a sprigged paper she had chosen herself, it gleamed newly in the overhead light, and it wasn't home. She switched off the light and went to the window to look out over the still black waters of the loch. Nothing moved; everyone was long since in bed and asleep. A white moon rode high in the sky, and Alison turned to Rusty. Only the soft gleam of her eyes betrayed where she lay and watched her mistress.

'Rusty, do you want to go OUT?' The magic word sent her up and quivering for action, and Alison laughed. 'Come on, girl, let's take a little walk by the loch.'

They crept quietly out, like two thieves in the night, and Alison left the door ajar so as not to disturb the others on their return.

It was cool, and she reached into the porch and lifted the nearest mac from a peg. Old and worn, it smelt of heather and tweed and fish, evoking instant memories of childhood fishing trips. She slipped it on as they went down the narrow path to the water's edge. Rusty, pleased at this unexpected treat after what must have been, to her, a very puzzling day, ambled along sniffing without much hope, for rabbits, and they reached the water's edge. Here Alison sat down on a giant stone, and waited for the peace and stillness to transfer itself to her. She needed something that would soothe away the restlessness of the day, and as they sat there, the calm and tranquillity reached her, and she was able to look around.

The loch was beautiful by day. Now, with the night upon it, it was breathtaking. The hard clear moon bathed everything with its cold unearthly light, lending a shimmering beauty to the water, and etching the trees in stark blackness against the backcloth of the sweeping hills. Everything was contrast, deep deep shadows, ghostly whiteness. And the only sound was the faint shush of the water, so near that Alison could reach out and touch it if she wished. She sat and looked, and knew that whatever else happened, nobody could take this away from her. This she would have, locked away in her heart, for the rest of her life.

It was time to go. It was gradually getting colder, and the mac was too old and worn to give much warmth. Alison stood up and called Rusty softly, and the dog ambled to her side. Then as she started walking, she found they were going in the direction of Courthill.

'Why not?' Rusty looked up startled as she said the words aloud. One last look around, with the house empty and waiting, might be what she needed to shake herself out of any self-pity. Just one last look to say good-bye as well. After tomorrow it would never be the same again.

Gently, footsteps quietly crunching on gravel, they made their way along, and Courthill loomed up grey and ghostly in the moonlight, the windows cold and yellow, catching the reflected light with blank expressionless eyes. It looked deserted, as if they had run away and left it alone. Alison walked up the steps to the front door, and it opened at her touch. They walked in, and the door creaked slightly, a lonely sound. The bare boards looked dusty in the gloom, and Alison walked quietly across and opened the lounge door. Here the moonlight slanted in, the elongated shape of the window cast across the floor in cold yellow, showing the shabbiness and emptiness starkly and clearly. Something had gone with the moving out of the furniture, some spirit that had kept the house alive.

It was like an empty shell. She looked at Rusty, and then knelt down and buried her face in the dog's fur.

'Oh, Rusty,' she whispered. 'It's not ours any more.' Rusty whined softly, and her tail drooped. Hot tears filled Alison's eyes, and spilled out into the dog's golden coat as she held her. She should not have come, she knew. It had been a mistake to return. It was all over. The memories came jostling then, of Niall MacBain's words so long ago, words that he had tried to pretend didn't matter the other day – that the house should really be his. And now it was. And over all that came the other more recent, even more painful and puzzling memory; when Johnny had told her of Niall's words to him on the night of the dance. They had meant nothing, said by a youth, perhaps as an excuse to fight, and yet somehow they had been frightening, almost prophetic – almost as if . . . She held her breath, shocked at the thought of what Niall might have intended Johnny to think, then she closed her eyes in despair.

It was best forgotten now and put to the back of her mind with all the other memories.

'Come on, Rusty.' It was time to go, and this was good-bye. Unsteadily she rose to her feet, and then Rusty growled low in her throat, and Alison froze as she heard the soft opening of the front door, footsteps across the bare boards in the hall—

'What on earth!'

Her first thought was: how absurd that he always turns up just as I'm thinking about him – followed quickly by revulsion.

'I'm just going,' she said coldly. She wished that she hadn't been crying, but at least he couldn't see.

'Come on, Rusty.' He stood in the doorway, and she could see him only hazily because of the shadows, and because her eyes were sore from weeping. Then, as she saw him reach out a hand towards the switch, she said: 'Don't – don't switch it on, please.'

His hand paused, he let it fall to his side, and perhaps he guessed, for he said more softly: 'I wasn't sure if they would work anyway.'

'Oh no – yes, I mean,' she stammered. 'They're coming to read the meter tomorrow.' She went towards him. 'Excuse me.'

'What's the hurry?' His voice held a note of grim amusement, as if he knew, and she answered: 'I can't stay.'

'Can't – or won't?'

She began to experience that odd breathlessness again, almost a feeling of claustrophobia. It made her angry – with herself mainly, but with him as well, for it was as if he had a measure of control over her actions, and she resented that. She snapped:

'It doesn't matter, does it? I'd just like to get off *your* property.'

'Then why come on it in the first place?' he asked quietly.

'I don't expect you to understand, so I don't intend to explain. Will you please let me pass?'

'In a minute. I came to see if everything was locked up. There's a band of tinkers camping by Donnie's Barn, and some rough-looking ones among them. I thought maybe a locked door would be safer if one of them was out looking for rabbits.'

'Then lock up. I'm going.'

'I'll walk back to the cottage with you.'

Alison moved away quickly, not knowing why. 'I'm not afraid of the tinkers. They're harmless enough,' she said.

'Are they? Have you met any at night?'

She laughed. 'No, and I won't now. Anyway, I'd feel safer with them than with *you*.' And she went past him, pleased with her parting shot, clicking her fingers for Rusty to follow. As she ran down the steps, she saw the light go on, and turned her head to see him standing in the middle of the room, hands in pockets, just looking round as if weighing up. The encounter, plus the shock of his sudden arrival, had left her feeling weak. And she disliked him more than ever. What's the matter with me? she wondered. She wasn't normally so childish, yet with Niall MacBain it was as if she was constantly on the defensive. Alison recalled again the words Johnny had told her, because they must have been so deeply etched on his brain that they would never be forgotten. Niall MacBain, who never told a lie, had said them. He had taken everything else from her. In a curious, cruel way, she could almost believe that he would want her too. There he would be thwarted. Alison vowed silently that she would not allow him to touch her again, ever.

The days passed, and the cottage began to seem almost like home. The weather was bad, and as the men were working away in the house, there was little to be seen. Niall was there with them every day, and sometimes he got home in time to greet his son, and sometimes old

Fergus had to look after him. It distressed Alison to think of him being alone in the house with the old man – not that she imagined he would harm André, but because he was morose, spent all his days checking the racing results or walking to the phone box to call a bookmaker, she felt sure André would be lonely. It was too wet to play out. The fine misty Highland rain, more penetrating than any downpour, had been coming down for days, so that all André had to do was wait by the window hoping for his father's return.

One particularly bad day decided Alison. She stopped outside Niall's home and looked at the boy beside her. Niall's car was gone, a sure sign he was out.

'If your grandfather will allow you, André,' she told him. 'You may come home with me.'

He looked at her, and some of the silent misery went from his eyes. 'I will ask her?'

'Yes. "Him," André, not "her." Go on now.'

She watched him slip in at the open door, and waited. Alison had never spoken to Niall's father in her life, but she was shrewdly aware that he would allow her to look after his grandson if it meant a bit of peace for him.

A few moments later the boy ran out and got back in the car.

'She – he says it is all right. My daddy is at the big house. I may go.'

'Fine.' Alison started the car.

Her first task was to let Niall know where his son was, to save him a fruitless journey home, so she stopped the car by the back door of Courthill, and telling André to wait, she went in.

It was strange to see the kitchen bare, without Jessie working away, and all their possessions gone. The only evidence of occupation were milk bottles, beakers and sugar on the bare table.

Faintly she heard a tuneless whistle, and even more distantly, the sound of hammering. She went into the hall and called: 'Anybody there?' The whistling and hammering stopped, then there were footsteps, and Johnny appeared at the top of the stairs, wearing plaster-smeared overalls. He began to walk down, his heavy shoes clattering on the uncarpeted stairs.

'Hello, Alison. Did you want something?' his smile was pleasant and warm.

'Hello, Johnny. It's your boss I'm after. Is he here?'

'Och, him.' He nodded behind him. 'Aye, he's away up in the attics. Will I give him a message for you?' He stood at the bottom of the stairs, very close, and Alison was strongly aware of his eyes upon her. She smiled at him. He was good-looking, nice and so different from the brooding man who had taken over her home that he seemed, in contrast, positively delightful. And one more thing her instinct told her. He was very much attracted to her. It was useless to try and ignore it, for he made it very clear. There was nothing wrong, she told herself, in enjoying it, and basking a little in the warmth of a masculine smile.

Then a strange thing happened. Johnny had a smear of plaster on his forehead, and a trace was over his eyebrow. Alison blinked, almost feeling it going in his eye, and lifted her hand. 'Stay still,' she said, and tweaked it away. As she tried to take her hand away, he put his own over hers.

'Thank you,' he said softly, and bent to kiss her palm. She was about to pull her hand away when a movement caught her eye and she saw Niall appear silently at the top of the stairs. Suddenly, on an impulse she couldn't explain, she stopped resisting, and as he kissed her hand, laughed lightly, eased her hand free, and looked up. She caught sight of Niall's face, and drew breath sharply. Anger flowed out of him in almost visible waves – and she suddenly remembered that other time so long ago.

Then he broke the sudden silence. His voice was quite calm and level, deceptively so, for Alison seemed to detect a ragged edge of anger in it.

'Did you want me? I saw your car.'

Johnny turned slowly, realizing they weren't alone, and she answered: 'Yes. It was such bad weather, I brought André here with me.'

'Thank you. I hadn't realized the time. I'm sorry.' Everything was well under control again.

'He'll be quite safe at the cottage until you want him. Your father knows.'

'Right. If you're sure – if he's any trouble, bring him over, I'll mind him here.'

'He won't be.' Alison turned to Johnny, and saw the spark in his eyes as she smiled at him and said: 'If you'd like to come over in a few minutes, I'll make you all a pot of tea.'

'Och, that will be fine. All right with you, Niall?'

Niall nodded, then vanished, and Alison realized something at that moment that gave her an indefinable sense of well being.

That innocent, harmless gesture of Johnny's had made Niall angry. Alison didn't know why, yet it was so. He disliked her, yet he objected to the other man's mildly flirtatious action. As she went out again through the kitchen, she smiled to herself. If she was right she had a weapon – a small one, but a weapon for all that – in her armoury in the battle against the loathed intruder. She liked Johnny, and there would be no harm in flirting a little with him. His heart was virtually indestructible, made of cast iron, if the various village maidens that Alison had gossiped with at different times were to be believed. As she ran out to the car, she thought of Meg. How she would enjoy hearing about it all! Alison began to hope that she and Bill would come up soon to Shielbaig. Meg would appreciate the slight tinge of irony so well.

Somehow, imperceptibly, it slipped into a routine, Alison's bringing home André every day. She didn't mind at all. Nor did Jessie or her mother, who both liked him in their own different ways. Jessie had decided, when she had first met him, that he needed feeding up – and set to to do just that. Both Mrs. Mackay and Alison had to admit that it showed results. His thin cheeks grew plumper, and a more healthy colour, and he enjoyed her fussing. And her mother constantly sketched him in her spare moments, thought his bone structure was 'superb', and was determined to paint him when she had time. Alison just watched, knowing, yet not daring to admit that she was growing to like him just a little more with each day that passed. She hated herself for her weakness – it could only lead to unhappiness when the inevitable separation came, as come it would – yet she could not deny her feelings, which were matched only by her dislike for the person closest to André, his father, Niall.

Another problem approached – the holidays. For six weeks the school would be closed, and André would be virtually alone, for Niall was now working hard every day at Courthill, and almost certainly could not spare the time to look after his son as he should be looked after. Alison mentioned her fears to Jessie on the Thursday before school finished. André was outside in the garden, throwing a stick for Rusty to retrieve, without much success, for although the two were now good friends, Rusty felt that collecting sticks was rather beneath her dignity, and made it plain.

'Well, child, what do we do?' Jessie asked, busily making sandwiches for the men at the house. Since the day of Alison's encounter with Johnny that had so displeased Niall, Jessie had kept them supplied with hot lunches, and tea and sandwiches at four-thirty. Niall insisted on paying for this service, saying that it saved them a lot of time, which it undoubtedly did. Yet Alison felt slightly uneasy about it. It was one more small encroachment into her life. Jessie enjoyed looking after them. She liked both Johnny and Niall, and Alison, having seen the way they behaved towards her, knew why. She had come in late for lunch one day, and was at the kitchen door before she realized that Jessie wasn't alone. As she was about to go in, she heard Niall's voice: 'You cook like an angel, Jessie. If only I were twenty years older—' and Jessie's rejoinder, tart, but with that slight hidden laughter Alison knew so well: 'Ach, away wi' your flattery!' She had gone in then, unwilling to eavesdrop, obscurely angry, and seen Jessie's sparkling eyes as she had handed Niall the lunch for the four of them. They had both looked around, and the smile had slowly vanished from Niall's face at the sight of Alison. He'd nodded, said coolly: 'I'll away now. Thank you, Jessie,' and had gone. Alison came back to the present to realize that Jessie was waiting for an answer.

'What will we do?' she shrugged. 'What can we? You know I'd willingly have him here, but—' she stopped, and bit her lip, unable to finish.

'Aye, I understand.' Jessie's eyes were kindly as they rested on her. 'It's difficult for you. Still, if your mother or I were to suggest we'd have him—'

'Would you?' Alison's face gave her away.

Jessie nodded slowly. 'I will. Alison, you mustn't let yourself get too fond of the boy, you know—'

'You don't need to tell me. I've already worked that one out for myself. How can I be like this, Jessie, tell me? Hating his father so, and yet with André – oh, I don't know.' She leaned on the table and put her hand on her chin. She sighed heavily.

Jessie's blue eyes were bright with concern, and something more, that Alison didn't understand. 'Are you sure?' she asked softly.

'Sure of what?' Alison was puzzled.

'That you really do hate Niall MacBain. Hate is a very strong word, you know.'

'Then dislike intensely will do. Yes, I am sure.' She looked up at Jessie, startled, as the meaning sank in. 'What exactly do you mean?' she added slowly.

Jessie gave a small shrug and busied herself cutting the sandwiches. 'Ach well, never mind, just an old woman's fancy. Only—' she stopped and pursed her lips.

'Only?' Alison asked suspiciously, and something in

the air brought a catch to her breath. 'Tell me, please.'

'Well, it's just that – I don't think Niall dislikes you quite as much as you try and make me believe—'

Alison gave a disbelieving snort, but Jessie went on: 'No, it's true. One day he came in to return the tea things, and you were playing in the garden with André.' She paused, and Alison said: 'Go on.'

'And he went to the window and watched you, and I saw—'

'Yes?' Alison could hardly breathe. She was almost frightened of what Jessie might say.

'I saw the expression on his face. He didn't look hard any more. He looked – almost gentle.' Jessie gave a little smile. 'And he looks very nice when he's gentle.'

'It was André he was looking at,' said Alison firmly.

'No. That's what I thought, until I went over to the window. And he was watching you.'

'Then he must have had a mental blackout,' she said cruelly. 'He loathes me as much as I do him, Jessie. Believe me, the feeling is mutual.' But something had stirred inside her at the words, something she could only suppress, and bury in the furthest recesses of her mind. I don't want him looking at me at all, she said inwardly. Gently or otherwise.

Jessie finished the sandwiches and slipped them into a large polythene bag. Then she picked up the teapot, and Alison said:

'I'll take them over.'

'But—' Jessie's eyebrows nearly vanished in surprise.

Alison laughed, back to normal again. 'I'll be giving them to Johnny or the Camerons. I like Johnny.'

And she picked up the things before Jessie could say any more. There was no need to call out when she went into the hall at Courthill. Johnny was coming down the stairs as she pushed open the door. He saw her and took the last few steps two at a time.

'I was just now coming over,' he said. 'Here, let me take that heavy teapot.' And he reached out and took it from her hands.

'Where are the beakers?' she asked.

'In the kitchen. I have a notion they need rinsing,' and he looked hopefully at her, making Alison grin.

'All right, I'll do them.'

'Come away, then.' He strode off, and she followed. She could hear distant hammering from upstairs, and wondered how the work was going on. As they reached the kitchen, she said: 'I'll help you carry these up. I'd like to see how much you've done.'

'That will be a pleasure,' he smiled slowly, watching her as she carried the beakers to the sink. 'I'll show you round.'

Alison returned them to the table, he added milk and sugar, and asked as he did so: 'Are you going to the games next week?'

'I wouldn't miss them for anything. And you, Johnny, are you going?'

'I am. There's the dance afterwards. You've not forgotten that?'

Alison smiled. 'No.' She knew suddenly where his questions were leading. To give her time, she said: 'What are you entering for?'

'The shinty match for one, of course. We're a player

short. How fit are you?'

She shook her head, laughter bubbling through. 'No, thanks! I played it once, and was covered in bruises for weeks after. That's one game I prefer to watch.'

He smiled, his eyes never leaving hers. 'I was only joking, Alison. It is too rough. But you'll maybe go in for something?'

'Perhaps. I usually do. I have seven small supporters, even if I win nothing.'

'Then you'll have another,' he took a sip from his beaker. 'Unless I'm in the same race as you, of course, in which case it's every man for himself! And the dance – you'll save some for me?'

'All right,' she smiled. 'If you wish.'

'I do wish.' He picked up two beakers and the packet of sandwiches. 'Let's go, or I might forget my promise.'

As they went to the door she looked at him, bewildered. 'Promise?'

'My promise to myself. Not to kiss you without invitation.'

'Oh!' She went through the door first, saving herself the necessity of hiding her grin. It seemed that she would have no need to manoeuvre Johnny into anything if she wished to test her theory about Niall Mac-Bain. In fact – and the thought came to her suddenly, startlingly; he was already well ahead of her. She would have to be very careful not to burn her fingers, she decided, playing with that fire.

CHAPTER SIX

NIALL was working with the Camerons on the first floor. Alison and Johnny carried the tea and sandwiches in to them, and she looked round what had once been the largest bedroom, the one shared by her parents until three years ago. Only now it was different.

Devoid of furniture, it looked very bare, and smaller, with a dividing wall making it into two rooms. The walls were stripped of paper, and had a curiously naked air. The elder Cameron, Laurie, was smoothing plaster over the newly bricked up fireplace, while his brother Ian burned paint from the window-frames with a blow-torch. They looked round as she entered, and stopped work to greet her with shy nods.

Johnny called out to Niall, the hammering from the next room stopped, and he came in, running his fingers through his thick black hair.

'Hello,' he said briefly, then seeing what she had brought: 'Thank you.' Before Alison could say anything, Johnny asked him: 'Can I show Alison round? She'd like to see our work.'

Niall moved towards the tea, then looked at her, his glance devoid of expression. 'Of course. Mind the door to the kitchen upstairs. It needs tightening.'

'I will. Come on, Alison.' As he went through the doorway, Johnny's hand rested for a moment at her waist, as if to guide her into the corridor. Alison wondered, childishly she knew, if Niall was watching.

They went up the stairs and into the first attic on the small narrow corridor. She stood still, looking round, seeing it empty for the first time in her life – save for Pegasus, the old rocking horse that now belonged to André, standing in a corner draped with an old sheet. Without the accumulation of rubbish that had filled the attic for years, the room was so much larger that it was unbelievable.

Here again the walls were stripped bare, the fireplace was bricked in and plastered, and the windows were devoid of paint. Alison looked at Johnny. 'It's so – different, somehow,' she said.

He nodded, and gave a little smile. 'Aye, it is. Wait until you see the rest.' He took her arm. 'Come and look.'

Dazedly she followed his lead into the others. It was the last one which showed the most startling change. They had just come out of the fourth attic, already nearly transformed into a bathroom, and Johnny carefully eased open the last door, and said: 'This is the kitchen.'

Then Alison realized. As she looked round the room, now with sink unit, built-in cupboards and cabinet, she asked: 'Is this where Niall and André are going to live?'

He nodded, looking at her coldly. 'Aye. Did you not know?'

'No. I thought—I imagined he might let someone else manage it for him—'

'Ach, no. He'll run the place himself all right. This floor is self-contained. He'll have a nanny for André, to live in—' her head shot up involuntarily, and anxiety flared in Alison as she thought of Jessie. '—and he'll be downstairs looking after the guests. I think he'll put this place on the map.'

He paused, then added quietly: 'And whether that's a good or a bad thing remains to be seen.'

'Well he should have no trouble when the road's built,' she said. 'Look at Aviemore.'

'It's not definite,' he watched her as if slightly puzzled. 'It's little more than a rumour, and you know how long anything takes up here.'

Alison looked round. 'It doesn't seem to take him long to do anything.'

'That's true.' He began to laugh. 'You hate his guts, don't you?'

'Do I make it so obvious?'

He shook his head, his smile dry. 'No, but I'm perhaps more sensitive where you're concerned. I like him – in spite of the fact that he beat me up years ago – over you.' The last two words were so softly spoken that she barely heard them. She looked at him, a brief flare of anger sparking in her eyes.

'I asked you not to mention that again.'

He put up his hand as if to ward off a blow. 'Whoa, sorry,' he gave a low whistle. 'My, but you're pretty when you're in a temper!'

'I am not in a temper,' Alison said very slowly.

'No, of course not,' he grinned. 'I never argue with a lady.'

'Oh, Johnny,' she was unable to hold back the smile, 'you're incorrigible!'

'If I knew what that meant, I might feel insulted, so I won't ask.' He held out his hand. 'Come on, I'll show you what we've done downstairs.'

'I'll follow you in a minute.' Something had just

struck her about all the cupboards, and she wanted to examine them more closely.

'Then I'll drink my tea before it goes cold.' He went out, and added: 'Mind the door.'

'I will,' but she wasn't really listening. She was crouching down by the long row of superbly finished cupboards with their sliding doors. Gently she pushed one open, and it slid smoothly along the groove. Alison moved her hand down its surface, admiring the craftsmanship that had gone into them. Then she knew what had made her pause. There was no maker's label anywhere, and she wondered if Niall had made them himself. He had always been top of the class in woodwork, much to Alec's chagrin, and even Alison had secretly admired the things he had made and painted himself. Intricate cigarette boxes, carved stools, even a child's chair had come from those skilful boyish hands. She stood and went to go out, taking one final look back as she opened the door wider – and remembered Johnny's warning just a fraction of a second too late. Even as she realized that no door should feel so loose as this, and tried to step out of the way, it toppled towards her, and she screamed as the weight came down, pushing her over backwards so that she sprawled full length on the floor with the heavy door on her legs.

As she lay there dazed, she heard as if from a great distance the sound of steps pounding up the stairs, and she tried to pull herself up, but in vain. The next moment Niall's face swam into view, then Johnny's, and the weight disappeared as if by magic. The tears of pain blurred Alison's eyes so that she couldn't see clearly, but it seemed to her that it was Niall who knelt then beside her, who said: 'Alison, can you hear me?'

She blinked rapidly several times, and stiffened at his touch, feeling his strong arms beneath her back as he eased her up.

'Yes, I'm – I'm all right.'

He turned his head slightly. 'Johnny, a cloth – plenty in the third-bedroom – soak it well—' Johnny had gone before he finished speaking, and Alison frowned. 'But I'm not—'

'Ssh! All right, stay still. I've got you. How did it happen?'

'I told Johnny to go. I wanted to look at the cupboards, and he w-went. He warned me about the door, but I d-didn't listen, I'm sorry.'

Then, to her utter dismay, she burst into tears. Loathing herself for the show of weakness in front of the enemy, she tried to gulp them back, but it only made things worse.

Then she saw her leg and gasped at the sight of the blood welling out and spreading over her ankle.

'No, don't look. It's not as bad as it seems. You must have caught it on the fastening.' Suddenly, he put a firm hand on her chin, and twisted her to face him. 'Can you sit up?'

Alison nodded, one half of her mind registering the rather surprising fact that Niall MacBain was not being hard or ruthless, or anything else she associated with him, but unexpectedly gentle.

The other half was busy with the pain from her leg; pain that throbbed mightily, making her gasp.

Johnny appeared carrying a cloth, well soaked. Niall looked at him. 'Wrap it round. It will do until we get her home.' He lifted her up a little more, his hand firm round the middle of her back. She winced as the cold cloth went on, but it was done a moment later, and Niall nodded. 'Right. Now, get over to the cottage, and tell Mrs. Mackay or Jessie that I'm bringing Alison over – and to keep the boy out of the way.'

Johnny looked at him. 'Do you want any help?'

'No, I can manage. Just prepare them. I'll follow in a minute.' Johnny vanished, and they were alone.

'Sit up,' Niall ordered. 'I'm going to tie that cloth so that it doesn't fall off,' and he pulled a handkerchief from his pocket and bound it round the makeshift bandage, then tied it in a knot. He looked at Alison with a grin. 'I'm not a doctor, but it will do.' Then, more slowly: 'Alison, I'm sorry this happened.'

She shook her head, still fighting tears, not knowing why. 'It was my own fault. I was careless, that's all. Don't b-blame yourself or Johnny, please.'

He stood up and looked down at her. 'I'm going to carry you home now. Just lie still – I shan't drop you.'

He bent and eased his arms carefully under her knees, and arms, then picked her up as easily as if she weighed as little as his son. In a very impersonal voice he said:

'Put your arm round my neck. Comfortable?'

She obeyed him and answered: 'Yes, thank you.' It was odd, but now that the immediate urgency was over, so did the temporary truce that the emergency brought about seem to vanish too. Alison went tense as she realized just precisely what was happening. Then his voice came abruptly: 'Relax.' There was a trace of harshness now. So he had noticed it too! She tried to, but a silent promise she had made to herself returned to

122

mock her. She had vowed never to let him touch her. Alison breathed deeply, trying to control the weakness that threatened, and they made their slow way down the stairs, along the corridor, and she was aware of the utter silence as they passed the room where the Camerons were. They would be watching, and wondering.

Then down again slowly and into the hall, cold and bare and empty. He glanced at her as they neared the front door. 'Are you all right?'

'Yes,' she answered, but she could scarcely breathe. Odd how it was starting again, but he was so close – too close for comfort. His face was only inches away, the face that she had told Jessie reminded her of a pirate's. She tried to slow her breathing, but it was difficult, and she prayed that he could neither hear nor feel the pounding of her heart. Deep tan, and dark hair, so dark, so near, and she couldn't take her eyes away from him. His chin was stubborn. She had never noticed before, never wanted to, just how obstinate and strong it was. He had cut himself just underneath it, she could see that clearly – dried blood in an inch-long line. Cut himself shaving that morning, and already with a faint shadow of beard showing again through the tan. He was so dark, that was why they had called him Black Niall, and the name suited him now, more than ever. Alison began to shiver helplessly as they went outside, and he mistook it and said: 'We'll be home in a minute, you need a warm drink.' But she couldn't tell him that it wasn't cold – it was fear. Fear of this dark stranger who had come back into her life so suddenly and was threatening it in so many different ways.

Jessie was so concerned that Alison had to reassure her that she was fine, and that there was really nothing wrong with her at all. Niall, seeing the old woman's anxiety, had taken complete charge, asking for bandages, antiseptic, and water. As Alison protested, weakly, that she would manage, he looked at her, once, with that very level grey glance, and she subsided. Useless to fight him. The only thing he allowed was her protest about Jessie's decision to go and fetch her mother from the studio. 'No,' he said, smiling a little as if to reassure Jessie. 'Alison says her mother need not come back, and I think she's right. But please, Jessie, I think a cup of tea would be very welcome.' And he bent down and removed the blood-stained cloth from Alison's leg, glancing swiftly at her as she drew breath. She was on her bed, and he had had Jessie bring in a towel so that the blood from the cut wouldn't mark the coverlet. Now, as he hesitated, she looked at him.

'What is it?'

He gestured with his hand. 'Your stocking.'

'They're not stockings,' she answered, 'they're tights.' And some spark of mischief drove her to add: 'So what are you going to do?' And let me see you get out of *that*! she added silently, waiting for his discomfiture. He knew. A glint of that quick temper showed for an instant, but was swiftly repressed.

'Lie back.' And she did, waiting for him to leave the room, knowing that he wouldn't dare . . .

The next moment the unbelievable happened. Alison felt Niall's hands slide under her skirt, up her hips, and then the tights were being pulled gently down, down her legs. Gasping, she struggled into a

124

sitting position, hot colour flooding her face as she stared first at him, then at her tights, now over her ankles. 'Oh! How dare you do that – you – you—!'

And Niall looked at her, unmistakably smiling. '*You* dared me, remember? I've already told you how I react to threats – and dares.' He deftly eased the tights off, but she winced with pain.

'Sorry.' He flung them over the chair and began to clean the cut on her leg. Alison lay back, her heart thudding, emotions very mixed, face still burning. It was she who was embarrassed, unbearably so. Her sides were on fire where his hands had touched, only lightly, but nevertheless in a most expert manner. She turned her head away, hearing Jessie come in, hearing her say:

'Shall I ring for the doctor?'

Feeling cool ointment being pressed on her leg as he answered:

'No, Jessie. It's a very shallow cut, a clean flesh wound. The antiseptic and the ointment will be sufficient.' Then he was tying the bandage round, and Alison opened her eyes to see Jessie hovering over her, lined face filled with worry, and love.

Alison smiled at her reassuringly. 'I'm fine, really I am. And I'd love that cup of tea.'

'Aye, well, come on now, sit up.' She put the steaming cup on the bedside table and plumped Alison's pillows. 'There now! And there's a cup for you in the kitchen, Niall, and a very worried wee boy.'

'Let me wash my hands, and I'll go and get it.' He picked up the bowl of water and went out. Jessie looked at Alison and nodded, an ominous gleam in her eyes. 'Mmphm!' she muttered. 'Well, I've seen some

enemies in my time, but that one takes a bit of beating.'
For a dreadful moment Alison thought she had seen
him take off her tights, and began: 'What do you—'

'You know fine well! Poor man was worried sick
about you, and you say—' she stopped as the bathroom
door opened, then put a finger to her lips. 'I'll away
and see to him. Have your tea, there's a drop of brandy
in it to warm you.' Then she was gone. Alison began to
drink. Would she ever forget the humiliation?

She phoned Meg later that evening, after having had a
short sleep. It was difficult to talk freely, for the phone
was in the hall, so near to where her mother and Jessie
sat in the living-room. Alison needed someone to talk
to, badly.

Her main purpose in ringing was to ask Meg to come
and visit the following weekend. They had brought the
twins up the previous year the week of the games, and
had all enjoyed themselves tremendously, leaving the
twins in the care of Alison's mother in the evening
while they went to the dance. Alison had already mentioned it to her mother, who was pleased at the idea,
and said it would do her good to have an interest.
Almost, Alison reflected, as she picked up the phone, as
if she thought I was bored.

Meg was delighted with the invitation, said that Bill
was out, but she was sure he would say yes, and that she
would ring Alison back. Then she added: 'And how's
the monster?'

'Well, it's a little difficult,' Alison began.

'Aha! You mean you can't talk freely?'

'That's right. We've moved into the cottage now.
It's a lot smaller.'

'I get you, loud and clear. Well, I'll phone you later, but I'm looking forward to it already. And we'll go to the dance in the evening?'

'Yes.'

'Marvellous. I love the atmosphere in that village hall. Can't wait! 'Bye, love, I'll call the minute Bill gets in.'

Alison put the phone down thoughtfully. She wondered what Meg would make of Johnny, who would undoubtedly be with them at the dance. She looked down at her injured leg and wondered if the bandage would be off before the following week.

The phone rang just as she was going to bed, and she picked it up, sure it would be Meg. But it was Johnny.

'Sorry to call so late, Alison. I wanted to know how you were.'

'Oh, Johnny! Thank you for phoning. I'm fine now.'

'Good. I was so sorry, Alison. I shouldn't have left you in the kitchen—'

'Nonsense. It was my own carelessness in not listening. You mustn't blame yourself.'

'Ach, well, it's nice to hear you're all right. I'll sleep well now! Shall I come over early tomorrow and drive you to school?'

She smiled. 'That's very kind of you, but really—'

'It's the least I can do. I insist – and I'll be at your home at quarter to nine in the morning. Sleep well, Alison, goodnight.' And giving her only time to answer his farewell, he hung up. Alison was oddly touched by his gesture. It was nice of him to offer, and it was clearly something that wouldn't have occurred to Niall

MacBain, she thought wryly.

But there she was wrong. She went to tell her mother who had phoned, and why, and Mrs. Mackay looked worried.

'Oh dear,' she said.

'Why? There's surely nothing wrong—' Alison began.

'Oh no, it's not that, but Niall came over when you were asleep. I'd just returned from the studio. He offered to come for you in his car in the morning, and I said you'd be all right. I hadn't realized—' she looked doubtfully at Alison's leg. 'Dear me, I hope he doesn't see Johnny taking you. It will look so bad.'

'Is that all?' Alison laughed. 'I don't mind if he does see me. *I* don't mind at all.' But as she said the words, she wondered if she was trying to convince her mother, or herself. The telephone's shrill ring saved her from further introspection.

It was Meg, and her words made Alison forget all about Niall's probable annoyance, as she assured her that she and Bill would be delighted to come down the following Thursday, with the twins, for a long week-end.

Alison went to bed happier than she had been for a long time.

There was never any work done on the last day of term. The prospect of six weeks' freedom was too heady to bear, and the children were full of mischief and fun as they all played 'Guess Who?' in which they all took it in turns to pose as famous people, and answer questions about themselves, until their identity was revealed. Alison smiled to herself a little as she sat back in a corner and listened, for once an onlooker in class. Little did they know, but this too, in a way, was helping them to learn, and as each 'character' has to whisper their identity to her beforehand, she was able to correct any glaring inaccuracies. She thought back to Johnny's arrival at a quarter to nine that morning. He had said he would come for her again at twelve to take her home, then back after lunch as well. He drove a battered Land Rover, and as noon approached, Alison watched for it coming up the hill. But it was Niall's car that she saw, and it stopped outside the school in a flurry of tiny stones from the road.

'Away to your lunch now, children,' she told them. 'André wait here. Your daddy has come for you.' They ran out, and she walked carefully to her desk for her bag as the school door opened, and Niall walked in.

She looked up as if surprised. 'Hello. You've come for André,' she said brightly.

'And for you,' he answered.

'Oh, but Johnny said—'

'He's very busy painting cupboards and fixing a door,' he answered. Then he looked at his son. 'Hello, André, have you been good?'

'*Sim, Papa*—'

'English, André. We must remember to speak English.' Their voices faded away as they went out, leaving her on her own. His tone when he spoke to his son was kind but impersonal. There seemed no warmth, no love. A fine tremor ran through Alison. It was as if they were strangers. How could Niall be so cruel to a little boy? And something else she had noticed subconsciously, which now came forward. When he spoke about André to Jessie or Alison, he always referred to him as 'the boy' or 'André', never 'my son'. As she went to the door, after a last quick look round, something more disturbing clamoured for her attention. Niall had never once spoken of his wife. If ever he had to refer to her, he said 'André's mother', but that was rarely. Surely, she thought, he could bear to speak of her now? But to do it so impersonally seemed heartless.

With a faint sigh, Alison closed the door and went to the car.

'Can you manage?' Niall asked.

'Yes, thank you,' she answered stiffly. She would have preferred to walk, but her leg was stiff and sore, and she wanted it to be all right for Meg's visit, and the games.

They drove home without speaking, except to André, who seemed unaware of the brittle atmosphere. Alison couldn't even for his sake, have forced conversation with the impossible man who sat beside her, his hands resting lightly on the wheel, those lean strong hands that had . . . Stop it! she told herself fiercely, hating him and herself – and she must have stirred slightly in her seat, for his glance flickered across, and he said: 'Leg hurting?'

'Yes,' she answered, regretting the lie immediately. But it made her scalp prickle, the way he seemed able to read her thoughts, almost as if he *knew* – oh, how she loathed him! And, too, for the casual way he treated André. He might have had a rough childhood, but that was no reason to inflict a similar one on his own flesh and blood, his son. She wanted to say it out loud – you are not fit to have a child – but she dared not, for there are some things that must remain unsaid. Once spoken they can never be retracted, and nothing is ever the same again.

She turned to look out of the window as they swept along the drive towards Courthill – his house. Instead of stopping at the back, as she expected, he took the narrower path to the cottage. Stopping outside, he turned to André. 'Jessie has told me she will give you some lunch – or will you have it with me in the big house?' As he spoke he was getting out, and Alison hastened to open her own door, unwilling for him to help her, or touch her again.

As she got out, so did André, and he put his hand in hers, as he looked up at Niall. 'Please, I like to have with Mees.'

A muscle tightened in Niall's cheek, but he merely nodded. It's all right, she thought wryly, I'm not going to try and take him from *you*. They walked in the front door, Niall behind them, and Alison called out to Jessie, who answered:

'I'm in the kitchen, Alison. Your mother's away in Strathcorran, picking material for the—' she came in wiping her hands on her apron, and saw Niall. 'Ah, you've come back. Good. You can take the food back to Courthill.' To Alison she added: 'Sit you down and rest the leg. I won't be a moment.' Alison walked in the kitchen after her, and sat by the table. Niall remained in the doorway, watching André, who had come to sit beside her. She hardened her heart. It was his own fault. Why should she feel sorry for him? But most oddly, she did. There was something in his face as he looked at his son that mystified her. Then, as Jessie handed him the huge covered dish and the plates, he became the hard, different man again.

'I'll be back at one-fifteen,' he said with a glance at

Alison.

'Yes. Thank you for the lift,' she said. But he had gone.

And so school closed for the holidays. Jessie told Alison that afternoon that André would be coming every day while his father was working. Her heart lifted absurdly.

'How did you ask him?' she said, wonderingly.

Jessie smiled, then chuckled. 'I came straight out with it. Told him he had to think of his son, and should I mind him, and he asked me if it would be too much trouble, because he intended having him at Courthill, and I told him it would be a crime, and that anyway we had friends coming down next week with two young children, and it would do him good.' She stopped to draw breath, then went on: 'And he insisted that he must pay me, so I told him you'd be helping me, and I was sure you wouldn't accept any money—' Alison nodded vigorously, '—and he said I was right there, and you were marvellous with him, and he could see the difference already.' She looked sternly at Alison. 'So he does appreciate something you do.'

Alison gave a little smile. 'He has a funny way of showing it.' André came in from the garden at that moment, carrying a bunch of assorted grasses, which he presented to her with a funny little bow before running out again. She sighed, looked at them, and went to fill a milk bottle with water. And the subject of Niall was dropped. But she felt a small glow, almost of satisfaction, at his words.

The holidays had begun, and they would have André, and next week Meg and Bill and the children would be coming to stay. The world began to look a little brighter.

Thursday dawned bright and sunny, and Alison awoke feeling fit and full of energy. Her leg was almost better. She had discarded the bandage the previous day, and as she dressed she looked critically at her leg. Only a slight scab was left of the cut. She began to look forward to the games on Saturday, and the dance in the hall afterwards. She had not seen much of Johnny during the week. Either Niall or the Camerons came over for the men's meals, and she had thought nothing of it. Then, on Thursday afternoon, she decided to take the tea across herself. She had made up, and wore a slim-fitting sleeveless dress in burnt orange, that fitted her to perfection, in readiness for her guests' arrival. On her feet she wore fawn sandals, and on her wrist a white bracelet that showed off her slight tan. She was breathtakingly beautiful – but quite unaware of the fact.

'My leg's fine,' she told Jessie as the housekeeper protested her offer. 'And I need some exercise.' She picked up sandwiches and teapot. 'I'm away.' She didn't see Jessie's amused smile as she went.

She walked in, heart beating a little faster than usual. The sounds came from upstairs, and she called out: 'Tea's here,' and waited.

She hadn't expected to see Niall appear, and for a moment was silenced, then as he came towards her, she said quickly:

'I wasn't sure if the cups would be upstairs.'

'No, they're in the kitchen.' He reached the bottom of the stairs, and his eyes were upon her as he walked nearer, softly taking it all in, the sandals, dress, hair, everything. She was suddenly embarrassed. The expression in those grey eyes was disconcerting, as if he were taking her apart and reassembling her, and deciding whether or not he liked the result. His hands came out and took the heavy teapot from her, and he said quietly: 'I'll take that.'

Alison turned to go towards the kitchen, very conscious of him following her, and of his eyes on her back and legs. She should not have come. She was making herself look foolish – the thought made her walk taller. Why should she give a damn for him? She marched into the kitchen, banged the sandwiches down on the table, picked up the beakers and went across to the sink. After rinsing them, she took them back to the table, said: 'There you are. I hope you can manage to carry them upstairs. I'm going now.' She wanted to hit him, and she wanted to cry, and above all, she wanted to get away. And he *knew*. She could tell by the smile that touched his mouth. Then he said, quite softly: 'Or shall I send Johnny down to help you pour?'

'I don't think you'd be able to spare him from his work, would you?' she managed to say.

The smile broadened slightly. 'Not really, but I'm sure you don't want to waste that dress on *me*!'

She walked quickly past him, leaning slightly to avoid any contact. She was determined not to start another argument, because with a man like him she couldn't win, and if she spoke she would only lose her temper, she knew. He had that effect on her. That and the stifled breathless feeling she hated, and which was coming back so strongly that she just had to get out in the fresh air.

He caught her just before she reached the door, and

put his arm across in front of her, just like that. 'What is it, Alison?'

'I didn't say that you could use my Christian name,' she answered shortly. 'And will you let me pass, please?'

'Forgive me, *Miss* Mackay. It was a slip of the tongue,' he bowed mockingly, but still blocked the doorway. 'Have I said something else that offends you?'

'Everything about you offends me,' she retorted. 'Don't worry, I shan't bring your tea again. I'll concentrate on looking after *your son* instead.'

She knew that she had hit the target by the expression on his face. He moved his hand, said: 'I'm sorry,' and turned away to go back to the table. Alison hesitated a moment in the doorway, then went out, back to the cottage. He'd asked for it, but having said it, she wished she hadn't. She tried to tell herself that it didn't matter, but she knew that it did. Somehow in those eight short words, she'd touched something deep inside him; had wounded him in a way she could only guess at. She looked back just before going out. He stood very still by the table. She had been wrong in one respect. Somewhere, he had a heart, after all.

It was like old times, like so many visits of Alison's to Inverness, but now they were in her own home. It was late on Thursday evening, and she and Meg sat by a warm fire in the living-room drinking cocoa and toasting their toes in the hearth. Bill and the twins were fast asleep in the tent outside. Alison had told Meg that they would have the children, but she had refused, and having seen the inside of the tent, Alison wasn't surprised. It was warm and cosy, and the boys lay sleeping snugly in their sleeping bags on low camp beds.

It was late, and both girls were tired, but there was so much that had to be told, and Alison was nearly at the end of it.

Meg listened completely fascinated, her cocoa growing cold, and as Alison reached the last, bitter words she had said in the kitchen of Courthill, Meg bit her lip.

'Was he angry?'

'No – it would have been better if he had been. I'm used to that,' Alison answered wryly. 'But he just turned away. Somehow I'd hurt him deeply – and it was almost frightening. I rushed out, and when he came for André later, I kept out of the way. Childish of me really, I suppose.'

'Mmm, well, he did ask for it.' Meg drank the remaining cocoa, and smiled. 'Enough of him. I'm dying to meet Johnny. He sounds a bit – well, you know!' And she raised one eyebrow meaningly, making Alison laugh.

'Oh, he is,' she assured her friend. 'You'll see him on Saturday if not before. I'm glad you're here, Meg. And the twins can play with André. He'll like that. He's a lovely boy.'

Meg gave her a look similar to one of Jessie's, and Alison smiled tightly. 'All right, don't say it, I know. Don't get too fond of him – I won't, don't worry.' She looked at the clock. 'Heavens, have you seen the time? It's nearly one. Bill will lock you out if you're not careful.' Giggling like two schoolgirls, they went into the kitchen, and Alison watched Meg safely into the tent before closing the door and going to bed.

The next morning when André arrived, Ian and Andrew, the twins, were playing ball in the garden with Bill, and Meg was with Alison in her bedroom experimenting with perfume. Niall had gone when they went into the kitchen, and Jessie nodded towards the window.

'Look at them,' she said. They watched the red-haired boys, still only three, talking to André while Bill waited in the background, arms akimbo, smiling at the serious manner of his sons as they introduced themselves.

'Why, he's not much bigger than my boys,' Meg whispered.

'I know,' Alison answered softly. 'Jessie's feeding him up, she says.' She looked round and grinned at Jessie, busily occupied with preparing lunch for twelve people. That was the wonderful thing about her. The more she had to cope with, the better she enjoyed the challenge. Now she was quietly humming under her breath as she peeled the potatoes. Many a time Alison had offered to help, only to be given a firm 'no.' Jessie worked better alone, and the results always justified her obstinacy. She did allow the girls to go to the village store, however, and Meg and Alison set off, leaving four males playing in the garden with Rusty sitting watching, and Mrs. Mackay at Courthill in her studio, busy with her new work. The only time Alison saw her was in the evenings, unless she came home for a cup of coffee during the day. She had changed. A new purpose lit her life as she matched and compared fabrics and shade cards for soft furnishings and carpets. Niall, it appeared, had given her a free hand in every way, and the confidence with which it had filled her was good to see. Good – and yet again Alison felt as if he were intent on taking everything away. Yet it was not something she could explain to anyone, even Meg. It was such a deep, intensely personal emotion that she could scarcely have put it into words. How much more would he buy? She still didn't know where his money – this fortune that had irrevocably altered her life – had come from. Meg was as fascinated as Alison about it. They didn't know then, as they walked to the shop in Shielbaig, that they were soon to discover the answer.

That evening they drove in Bill's station wagon to have a drink at the hotel in Strathcorran. The twins were safely tucked in Alison's bed, already in their sleeping bags for transfer on their return. The first person Alison saw as they walked in the hotel was Johnny, about to buy a drink. He crossed the crowded cocktail bar to them, a grin on his face. Alison introduced him to Meg and Bill, and was amusedly aware of Meg's subtle weighing up. She would, she knew have a full report on the way home.

Soon they were sitting together in a comparatively quiet corner, Bill and Johnny discussing football and cars, while Meg and Alison chatted, and occasionally joined in. It was pleasant, and rare, for her to have an evening out, and she was enjoying it more than she imagined. Then suddenly the conversation changed, and the men were talking about Courthill. Bill was interested in the work Johnny was actually doing, so he began to explain, drawing diagrams on the table with a forefinger as he described the layout of the house Meg and Bill knew so well. Bill nodded, interested, gave a low whistle as Johnny told him about the conversion of the upper floor into a self-contained flat. 'That will cost a lot, on its own,' he commented dryly.

'Och, he's loaded,' Johnny winked at Alison. 'I wouldn't mind a small share in that mine, would you, Alison?'

'Mine?' she echoed stupidly. 'What mine?'

'Do you mean to say you don't know about it?' It was his turn to look stunned. 'It's one of those tales that you wouldn't believe – except that it's true.'

Seeing their intent faces, he laughed. 'I'd better tell you, but first another drink. My round, I think,' and he vanished towards the bar, leaving the three of them looking at one another. A few minutes later he returned, sat down, and looked around.

'Are you sitting comfortably? Good,' he grinned. 'I've never had such an attentive audience. I—'

'Johnny!' Alison said warningly.

'Och, all right. Well, apparently Niall and his brother and two other sailors found themselves in a bar in Rio one hot summer evening several years ago. They were slightly – er – merry, and they got talking to a nice old man who told them this tale about the iron mine he owned, somewhere in the wilds of Brazil – but hard times were forcing him to sell, etcetera; a real con story, but as I said, Niall admits they were all slightly tiddly, loaded with money after months at sea, and the long and short of it is that they chipped in and bought this mine for a ridiculous sum – something like two hundred pounds in our money. The old man gave them some impressive documents, wrote them a receipt that was almost illegible, and remembered a very urgent appointment elsewhere. Of course they discovered they'd been well and truely "done" next day, when in the cold sober light of morning they took the certificates along to a police station.'

He paused, took a deep swallow of lager, and then went on:

'There they were told, with great amusement, that the mine was in fact a genuine one – but had been closer for years, was derelict, and certainly worthless.' He stopped and looked at them, and Alison knew by his smile that something big was coming, but couldn't see what.

'Go *on*,' urged Meg impatiently.

'Niall hung on to the papers, more for a souvenir than anything else, and as a reminder not to talk to strange men in bars. Then about three years ago, some prospectors opened up a rich new vein of iron in a mine a few miles away from theirs – and suddenly it wasn't worthless any more. It was in all the Brazilian papers. And the owners of the other mine were looking for the owners of their mine. Duncan was in Rio at the time, having left the Navy, and he contacted Niall, who went there with his "worthless bit of paper," and they sold their mine for a terrific sum – Niall didn't say how much – and the four of them shared it between them.'

He stopped and looked at their astonished faces. 'Yes, I know it's fantastic – but it's true.'

'So,' Alison breathed out slowly, and looked at Meg. 'So now we know!' All the suppositions and rumours had been as nothing compared to this modern fairy tale. And it was due to some old man in a bar that Niall now owned Courthill. Fantastic, as Johnny had said, but very true. She wondered again about his wife. He must have already been married when the fortune came, and André would have been a baby. Yet he, apparently, was still in the Merchant Navy, sailing the world. Something, somewhere didn't make sense. Alison knew she would probably never know. André never spoke about his life before coming to Shielbaig, and she would never ask him. Soon afterwards they finished their drinks and left, promising to see Johnny at the games the following day.

There was excitement in the air as they walked the following afternoon to Shielbaig for the games. These were held about a quarter mile past the village in a huge open field, and people came for miles around to compete, to meet old friends, and to indulge in that favourite Highland pastime – a good gossip.

The twins ran on ahead, full of energy, jumping and pushing one another, playing like a couple of puppies, themselves infected with the air of gaiety, though without knowing why. Alison wondered if they would see Niall and André. He had not been at Courthill that morning, but his car was outside his father's as they passed.

Cars, bikes and vans passed them, and Alison waved to everybody she knew, while Meg beside her kept saying: 'Don't forget now, when you see the monster – tell me.'

'I will. Besides, you'll know him from my description.'

Meg began to laugh. 'You made him sound like a black-bearded pirate! I keep looking for someone with a patch over one eye, and waving a Jolly Roger, but so far, I must admit—'

'You're an idiot,' Alison stifled her laughter. 'Can

you just imagine!' she looked sideways at her friend. 'Oh, Meg. I'm so glad you're here. You can't think what it's like, having no one to confide in. Jessie and my mother have gone over to his side, there's no other way to put it. Of course I'm glad that Mother has a new interest, but it's so—' she stopped, unsure of what she wanted to say.

Meg squeezed her arm. 'I know, Alison. I understand, truly I do. And I'd feel the same way about him, but—' and she bit her lip, her pleasant face troubled '—but even so, he sounds so – intriguing, somehow. Not like an ordinary man, but – well, larger than life.'

'He's that all right,' Alison agreed bitterly. 'And if you dare say he's good-looking, I shall personally strangle you!'

Both laughing, they walked into the field where already nearly a hundred people were gathered, with more coming all the time. Some were in small groups, others walking idly about, inspecting the various marked-off parts for the different races. The highlight of the afternoon would be the shinty match, after everything else was over. To the back of the field a large tent had been erected, waiting for the rush for cups of tea. The twins ran off screaming delightedly at having such a large field to play in, and Bill paused to let the girls catch up with him.

'I might have a go at the bicycle race,' he said with a grin, pointing to the pile of ancient bikes leaning against an old oak. Alison's mother and Jessie had said they would follow on, and Alison looked round from their vantage point near the tent, wondering how long they would be. She wondered idly if they had decided to come earlier than usual because of Niall. It would be the ideal place to let the whole world know that the feud was dead. And so she waited, watching, talking and listening to Meg and Bill, and keeping an eye on the twins who had been roped in for a jumping game with some pupils in another part of the field.

More people came, car doors slammed, urns were carried into the tea tent by self-conscious youths, followed by giggling girls. It was all the same as every year – yet there was one thing different, and so she waited, and watched.

Then she saw him. He stood by the entrance to the field, with André, and Alison touched Meg's arm lightly. 'He's there.' She saw Meg turn slowly, not making it obvious, saw her looking, then Meg turned back to Alison, her eyes wide. 'I don't believe it!'

'Don't believe what? Meg had her back to him, and Alison could still see him as he was greeted by an older man, then another.

And they stood talking, then André, seeing Alison, said something and tugged at Niall's arm, then began to run towards them.

'André's coming over, be careful what you say,' Alison warned, as the little boy reached them and looked up smilingly at her.

'Hello, André. The twins are over there,' she pointed. 'Do you want to go and play with them?'

He regarded her thoughtfully, then nodded, and streaked off to join the laughing crowd of children.

'I can't believe I'm really seeing *him* at last.' Meg turned casually round, looking everywhere, then at Alison. 'Will he come over and speak to you?'

Alison pulled a face. 'Not if he can help it, but if my

mother—' She stopped and waved, seeing them by the gate. 'She's here now with Jessie – and we'll soon see.'

It happened about half an hour later, when the games had begun, and they all stood round the perimeter of the field in an orderly crowd. The children's events were first, and they all clapped and cheered, and laughed, at their efforts in the races. Jessie was beside Alison, very smart in her best blue hat, lavishly decked with flowers. Mrs. Mackay stood beside her, small and elegant in a blue trouser suit. And Alison saw her wave, then heard her greet someone, and she knew it was Niall.

So it had happened. She had been right. And Meg would have her wish. Alison looked at her, oblivious to what was going on beside her as she watched Ian and Andrew hopping madly along in the race for tiny tots. She suddenly wanted very much to know what Meg thought about Niall MacBain, but she couldn't understand why.

CHAPTER SEVEN

MEG told Alison much later, at the dance, when Bill and Johnny had gone to join the fight for sandwiches and cups of tea. It was the first chance they had had of talking together since the games.

The noise around them was so deafening that anything they said would be quite private. Meg leaned across and said in Alison's ear:

'About you-know-who.'

'Yes, what about him?'

'You really think he's not attractive?' And Alison looked at her. There was one thing about her friendship with Meg. The two of them had never been able – or wanted – to be less than truthful in anything with each other. Now was the test. Grudgingly Alison admitted: 'Well, I suppose he's got a certain something.'

'I'll say he has! Honestly, Alison, you want your head feeling! Here was I imagining something really awful – you know – but he's so charming. You know when your mother introduced us?' Alison nodded, silent, waiting. 'Well, he looked at me with those grey eyes – it's immoral for a man to have eyes as sexy as that – and I had to try hard to remember that I'm a respectable married woman and mother!' Her eyes sparkled with humour, and Alison forced a little smile. 'And he was so – well, nice when he spoke that I had difficulty in reconciling him with this ogre who's so utterly vile to you.' She gave Alison a very keen look.

'In fact, if I didn't know you so well, I'd have thought you were making it up.'

Just then the men came back, effectively bringing an end to their conversation, but for the rest of the evening, as Alison danced with either Johnny or Bill, she remembered Meg's words. So her last ally had gone! She began to wonder, quite seriously, if there were something wrong with her. Perhaps they were right, and he was charming and wonderful, and it was Alison herself who saw him somehow through a distorted lens, one twisted by the feud, and what had happened in childhood, and a thousand other things that went to make a person. She remembered too the time in the attic, when he had steadied her with André, and the ridiculous sensation she had experienced then, of wanting him to hold her. That too, Alison had told Meg, and she hadn't laughed, as Alison would have expected, she had given a little mysterious smile. Perhaps I am a frustrated schoolteacher after all, she thought miserably.

Johnny's voice broke into her thoughts.

'A penny for them.' She looked back at him, aware that she had been miles – no, only one mile away, in that attic at Courthill.

'Sorry, Johnny. I was day-dreaming.'

'At eleven at night?' his arms tightened round her. 'You'll have to do better than that.' He skilfully avoided collision with another couple on the hot crowded floor, and swung her towards the door. 'Let's go outside for a breath of fresh air.'

'All right.' She knew it wasn't fresh air that was on his mind, but a numbness had come over her and she didn't really care.

Outside it was cool, and she shivered. Pitch blackness was all around them, but faint murmurings and stifled laughter told Alison they weren't alone. Johnny put his arm around her. 'Cold?'

'A little.' She knew he was going to kiss her, and she willed herself to enjoy it when it happened. They began walking round the side of the hall which vibrated with the enormous volume of sound bursting out. There was a bench somewhere round the back, and she imagined they were making for that, when . . . Suddenly his mouth came down on hers, his arms slid firmly round her, imprisoning her, and she found herself pressed against a tree, with Johnny leaning on her, wordlessly kissing her, pausing only slightly for breath. Alison tried hard to respond, to enjoy the warmth of his embrace, but in vain. Something froze her, held her back from answering the primitive emotions he tried so hard to arouse. After a few minutes, she pushed him slightly away, pretending to be flustered.

'Heavens, Johnny, you took me by surprise,' she whispered.

'Oh, Alison, don't torment me – you're so beautiful, come here—' and he tried to kiss her again, but she wriggled away.

'You're too dangerous,' she said, praying that Meg would look for them – knowing too that she wouldn't. 'A girl's not safe with you,' she protested, as his hand began moving up from her waist. She took hold of it and returned it to its orginal position.

Johnny's voice was husky with emotion. 'I've been wanting to kiss you for weeks, ever since that day, remember?'

'I remember.' If she could keep him talking and lead

him gently back to the hall . . . It had been a mistake to come out. There was no magic cure here for whatever ailed her, she realized. Nothing to take the ache from her, the pain of hating someone that everybody else thought so marvellous.

'And I've been wanting to ask you out, but I was afraid—'

'You afraid? I don't believe *that*.' They were moving in the right direction.

'Yes, I was. Och, I know what you're thinking. I'm no angel. But you're different, Alison. There's something about you – remote somehow. You're more beautiful, more wonderful than ever – och, I'm no good with words.' His hand tipped her chin and he kissed her more gently this time, almost sombrely. Then he released her, and although it was dark, she sensed the sadness about him as he murmured: 'You're not for me, I know that now, Alison. You are – I could fall in love with you. Perhaps for the first time in my life, I could truly love someone, but I know now—' and he stopped, and traced a line on her chin, gently. She knew he was deeply sincere. It moved Alison so that she softly kissed his cheek. There was no need for words. And she did not ask him what he had been about to say.

Slowly they walked back to the hall. Alison knew that Johnny would be different. He had changed in those few minutes outside – something had made him say what he did – and she realized there was more depth to him than anyone knew. Alison hoped sincerely that he would find happiness with a girl who would be able to love him as much as he deserved. But for her there would be nothing – she knew that now, quite suddenly.

Niall had told Bill on Saturday at the games that he was welcome to see the work at Courthill, and on Sunday morning the three of them went round. Alison's mother still had a key to let herself in, for the new door to the studio was not yet done, and her only entrance was through the house. Everything was quiet, almost eerily so as they walked through the hall, and Meg whispered:

'It's so different now,' looking round at the high bare walls, the uncarpeted staircase with its delicate wrought iron work, and the various doors leading off the hall.

Silently Alison agreed. Some of the pain had gone, and she could come into the house more easily every time. Soon she might be able to enter that front door, and it would be like going into a stranger's house. Maybe . . .

She showed them round the attics, knowing Meg's reaction to the conversion. She stood in the kitchen doorway and turned back to Alison. 'This will be really marvellous when it's finished – better than mine!' This with a sly look at Bill, who grunted, being too busy examining the cupboards to comment.

'I know,' Alison answered. 'It will be virtually a little house. I admit he's clever. He made those cupboards too.'

Meg looked at the door. 'Oh! So this is where—'

'Yes.' Alison pulled at the door. 'They fixed it straight afterwards. It was my own fault.' And suddenly she didn't want to talk about it any more. They went down, through the bedrooms, and then down to the ground floor, as yet unaltered. That would be done last, she knew. Bill was very impressed with the quality of the work. She then took them into the studio and showed them her mother's designs. Meg gazed wide-eyed at the picture of the reception hall as it would be. 'I'd be tempted to come here myself for a holiday,' she told her. 'Honestly, Alison, this place will be something special. Really, I mean it,' she emphasized, seeing Alison's face, which showed her disbelief.

Alison shrugged, said carelessly: 'Perhaps you're right. We'll see soon enough.' But inside, a pain stabbed her.

They went back home for lunch. Meg and Bill were leaving for Inverness the following day, and the girls had their last gossip that evening by the fire. They were both tired after the dance the previous night, and it was only eleven when they said good night to each other and went to bed. Alison was exhausted with something more than just a late night. An incredible weariness overcame her as she lay in bed looking up at the ceiling. What was the use of fighting any longer? She felt as if she were being swallowed gradually into a giant whirl-pool. Nobody would ever understand how she felt. It must be her. Something must be wrong with her. She turned her face into the pillow and wept.

The next two days were spent quietly at home. Some of the life had gone with Bill and Meg's departure on the Monday, and Alison felt restless, as if she wanted to get away. She avoided going near Courthill, and stayed away from the kitchen at the times Niall came for their lunch or tea. She took André for walks with Rusty, and enjoyed listening to his quaint English accent. He had begun to speak more, as if emerging from his shell, and told her a little of his flight to Scotland. But of his life before, he would not or could not speak, and Alison, longing to know, but not daring to ask, remained silent. It was nothing to do with her, she knew, yet there was a strange fascination in thinking of André's mother, and of what she had been like.

They walked for miles some days, and the weather remained sunny and pleasant, and everything would have been perfect if it hadn't been for the shadow that remained at the back of Alison's mind like a small dark cloud. There was nothing that would make it go away. Niall MacBain had come back for good. There was only one solution – for Alison herself to leave, and she loved Shielbaig too much to want to do that – yet.

On Wednesday she left André playing with Rusty while she went to the shop for Jessie. When she came back, he had vanished with Rusty and she set off to find them, knowing they would not have gone far. She set off down the garden, opened the small wicker gate at the bottom, and followed the route they usually took on their walks, the path that followed the loch round to Shielbaig. She stopped after only a few yards as she saw the tiny figure standing by the boat, which was pulled up on the shingle. Rusty sat patiently beside him, and then, seeing Alison, got to her feet and ambled across wagging her tail.

'I didn't know where you were, André,' she said. 'You mustn't leave the garden without asking.'

He looked at her, gave a little shrug, then said: 'But it is so quiet with no one to play with. I come only to see the boat. I like her very much.'

Alison smiled. 'Perhaps your daddy will take you out

in her to the island over there.' She pointed towards the tree-covered mound set serenely in the dark water.

'You will come if I do?' he asked, his eyes anxiously upon her. She ruffled his hair. How could she tell him?

'Perhaps,' she answered. 'Some day.' But she knew she would not. She held out her hand. 'Come on, we'll go back. Jessie will be worried about you. I think she's made some scones. You like those, don't you?'

He nodded, and they set off home. As they passed Courthill something made her look up, and it seemed that a man was standing at the upstairs window watching them. The sun reflecting off the glass made it impossible to see exactly who, but she had a feeling it was Niall. Without knowing why, she released the boy's hand. And deep down, the memory of those cruel hurtful words she had said stirred and returned to torment her, and she wanted him to see that she knew André didn't belong to her.

The next morning a letter arrived from the Education Committee. Couched in official language, it told Alison that at the breaking up of school for Christmas, it would close 'until such time as circumstances permit its reopening'. The remaining children would be transferred to Strathcorran, and taken by school bus. Alison would go there temporarily, until a transfer could be arranged. Even though she had half expected the news it still came as a considerable shock, and her mother saw her face as Alison read the letter at the breakfast table.

'Why, Alison, what is it?' She passed the letter across to her mother, who read it twice, as if disbelieving it.

Then she looked up, her face distressed. 'I'm so sorry. Did you know before?'

'I had a good idea, but I didn't want to worry you about it. You had enough to think about a few weeks ago, and I tried to push it to the back of my mind.'

'You should have told me, even so. Heavens, child, no wonder you looked so unhappy! Still, Strathcorran's not too far away – it's just that this is such a nice school.'

'Perhaps a miracle will happen before Christmas,' said Alison lightly. But she knew it wouldn't, and so did her mother.

She saw Johnny later on that day for the first time since the previous Saturday. Alison was coming out of the shop as he went in.

'I'll not be a moment,' he said, touching her arm lightly. 'Wait, and we'll walk back together.'

A minute later he caught her up, and stuffed two packets of cigarettes in his pocket.

'Now if I'd known you wanted them,' Alison told him, 'I would have got them for you.'

'Ach, never mind. And how would you have known, eh? You've been keeping out of my way all week,' he answered, grinning. He took the basket from her and held her arm.

'Johnny!' she protested. 'Have a care! Carrying my basket, and linking arms! The villagers will have us engaged if you don't watch out!'

'Let's give them something to talk about then. It's little enough they've got to do. Shall I kiss you as well?'

She quickened her step, well aware of watching eyes

as they passed the last few cottages. 'You wouldn't dare.'

'Wouldn't I?' he gave a low growl in his throat. 'Wait until we're nearly home, then see.'

She looked at him and smiled. Had he forgotten those words so softly spoken at the dance? She doubted it. Perhaps he had meant them at the time, and they had left her with a pleasant afterglow, which came back as they walked slowly along the road to Courthill.

His arm was warm in hers, his manner quieter than usual. They talked about the work, and of Meg and Bill, and the games. But one name wasn't mentioned. It was as if Niall MacBain didn't exist.

Through the greenness of the sheltering trees, along the narrow path to Courthill they went, and then, by the back door, they stopped.

'I'll come over for the lunch today, if I can,' he said.

'That will be nice.' Alison opened her eyes-wide. 'Such an honour!'

Something sparked in his own eyes, and as she half turned, putting out her hand for the shopping bag, he said softly: 'Alison?' and still held on to the bag.

'Yes?' She turned back, and his free arm came round her as he bent his head and gave her a slow gentle kiss.

As they broke apart she saw Niall MacBain come out of the garage, his arms full of wood. He looked, but said nothing, and then went into the house.

Johnny gave a low whistle, and smiled softly. ' 'Bye for now.' Then he too was gone, and Alison went on home. She was left with two questions to tease her. Had Johnny known that Niall would be in the garage? And had he then kissed her deliberately? There was no one to answer her.

For the rest of the day she busied herself making a dress. She had had both pattern and material for a while. André sat fascinated watching Alison as she snipped away at the material, a rich dark blue crimplene, then began to sew on the ancient but reliable machine. She was so busy that she nearly managed to forget the letter in the buff envelope behind the clock on the mantelpiece. Everything was so normal, uneventful, perhaps a little dull, that the work was an enjoyable change, and as she went to bed that night, she decided that she would finish the dress the following day. She couldn't know that her life would never be the same again after tomorrow.

There was nothing to warn Alison when she woke up on Friday that this was the day of destiny. André arrived at the usual time, and she caught a glimpse of Niall's back as he vanished out of the kitchen door. André ran to her and flung his arms round her legs in a burst of a delighted laughter.

'My *papai* will take me to the island tomorrow,' he told her; his accent was stronger in his excitement. 'She see us looking at the boat, and she will take.'

'There you are,' Alison smiled at Jessie, who watched them benignly. 'I said he would.' So it had been him at the window. Perhaps he had seen, or sensed, the longing in his son's eyes as he watched the boat at the edge of the loch.

'I ask her – him – if she take you, Mees, but she say no, Mees Mackay is too busy to come.' Alison saw Jessie purse her lips and turn towards the work that waited for her. And Alison smiled brightly at the boy, annoyed at the tremor at the corner of her mouth. 'Yes, I will be too busy, but perhaps one day I'll be able to.' She ruffled his hair. 'Well, do you want to take Rusty out, and then we'll start on my dress again?'

'Please, yes.' His eyes shone, and she stifled the lost eerie sensation that suddenly plagued her. She was pleased that Niall was beginning to take his duties as a parent a little more seriously.

The morning passed as did every other morning of the holidays. And every day André eased himself a little further into the fabric of Alison's life. Perhaps, she thought wryly as she drank her coffee at eleven, and watched him trying to make Rusty sit up for a biscuit, perhaps Niall will be pleased that the school is closing at Christmas. She bit her lip as the coffee cup jerked sideways, spilling the hot drink on her work table. She quickly mopped it up. What is the matter with me? she wondered. Alison knew she was tired, for she hadn't slept as well as usual for about a week, and her mirror showed paleness, and the faint smudges of fatigue under her eyes. A holiday would do her good, she knew, away from Shielbaig and everybody. But she didn't want to leave, for fear of what might greet her on her return. It didn't seem possible that Niall Mac-Bain could rob her of much more, but with him nothing was certain, and an unpleasant dream of the previous night returned suddenly with dreadful clarity even as she finished the last of the coffee. She dreamed that she had come home from school to find the cottage cold and empty. When she had called out, an answer had come from Courthill, and she had walked over, trying to go fast, but with weights dragging her feet

back. It was a struggle to reach the steps, to climb up
... and then she had seen her mother coming to the
door, as in the old days to greet her, and welcome her
in. She had run in, sobbing with relief, to look round
the newly decorated reception hall, and then she saw
the desk, and phones, and her mother's smart uniform.
Even as Mrs. Mackay smiled and shook her hand,
Jessie had come from the lounge, dressed identically,
and asked Alison if she would like a cup of tea, in the
restaurant ... and then she woke up, drenched in per-
spiration.

Of course it had only been a dream, and it couldn't
happen, but it was still too real for comfort, as were any
nightmares that took time to fade.

Her mother, yellow overalls spattered with paint,
came in for lunch and they all ate together in the
kitchen.

'They'll be knocking a hole in the studio wall,' she
told Alison as they finished their sweet. 'Then I'll have
my own door. I've been trying to move all the paintings
safely out of the way.'

'Can I help?' asked Alison. 'André and I could come
over this afternoon if you like.'

'Would you, dear?' She looked vague for a moment.
'There are such a lot to be moved – yes, that would be
fun. I don't see half as much of you as I would like, just
lately.'

'And I'll bring you some tea over at three-thirty,'
added Jessie. So it was arranged. And when lunch was
over, the three of them went back to Mrs. Mackay's
large untidy studio at the side of the big house.

They were so busy that Alison lost count of the time
until André said: 'Please may I have a drink?'

'Why, of course.' She looked at her watch. It was nearly four o'clock. 'It looks as if Jessie has forgotten us. Come on, we'll go and fetch something back.'

They set off through the conservatory, across the hall, and at any moment she expected to bump into Jessie gossiping with one of the men as the tea went cold, but the sounds of work continued upstairs, and they saw no one. Towards the cottage Alison began to run, hearing the faint whistle of the kettle, sensing that something was wrong. The kitchen was filled with steam; it billowed out through the open door and for a moment she thought it was smoke, until she realized it was from the kettle.

She ran in leaving André outside, heart thudding in sudden fear. She could see nothing for the steam that filled the entire kitchen and curled its way into the living-room. 'Jessie!' she shouted, pulled the hot kettle from the stove and switched it off, then flung open the window.

Then Alison heard the faint moan and her scalp prickled. As the air cleared she saw Jessie lying awkwardly on the floor, a fallen footstool beside her telling its own story.

She knelt and touched the old woman's forehead gently. 'Oh, Jessie dear! Don't try to move or talk. I'll get help.'

She ran to the frightened boy outside. 'Go and fetch your daddy,' she said. 'And my mother. You understand?'

'*Sim*.' Eyes wide, he turned round and scampered off, and Rusty came out of the living-room whining softly, with her tail well down. Alison knelt beside Jessie again, pulling a cushion from the kitchen chair and easing it beneath her head. She dared not look at Jessie's left leg which was twisted beneath her at an awkward angle, for fear that the dismay would show in her face. She prayed that Jessie hadn't broken it, and that help would soon come. Jessie clutched Alison's hand, her eyes filling with tears. 'I was getting down the tin of scones,' she said faintly. 'The stool was not steady, and the next thing I knew, I could hear the kettle whistling away.'

'I know.' Alison squeezed her hand. 'André has gone for Niall and my mother. I'll fetch you a blanket and some brandy.'

She covered her up and helped Jessie sip the warm liquid, and at that moment Niall, closely followed by Johnny, came in. It was so much like history repeating itself that Alison had a strange feeling that everything had happened before. It had, but very differently. Hers had been a trivial accident. This could be serious. And she saw by Niall's face as he knelt beside her that he thought the same. She stood up and went to Johnny. 'Does my mother know?' she asked, stiff-lipped.

'Yes. André went after telling us.' He came to Alison's side.

'You look white, Alison.'

'Yes. It's her leg. Look at her leg,' she whispered. Niall, kneeling beside Jessie, looked up at Alison.

'Is there a doctor still at Strathcorran?' he asked.

Johnny answered. 'Aye, shall I away and fetch him?'

'No. We'll take Jessie in my car to save time. Drive it up here, Johnny, as near as you can to this back door. Alison, I want blankets and pillows.' And then to Jessie, he added: 'Don't worry, love. You'll soon be all right. I'm used to this,' and the faint answering smile on her face, twisted by pain, wrenched at Alison's heart. She hurried to do Niall's bidding, aware of Johnny also leaving.

Ten minutes later they were gone. Mrs. Mackay had insisted, very firmly, on going with them, and Alison was left with André to await their return.

She made a cup of tea for the Cameron brothers, and took it over, glad of something to occupy her mind. She still saw Niall and Johnny carrying Jessie out to the car as carefully as if she were made of spun glass, and she knew that Niall was right, as always. He had taken charge as if used to it, and everything had gone smoothly. She had watched the car roll gently down the path, and had then gone back to reassure André.

That was the worst part, waiting for someone to come back, and not knowing. Half an hour later the phone rang shrilly, and Alison went to pick it up, her hands suddenly clammy.

CHAPTER EIGHT

JOHNNY'S voice came over the line, and he was phoning from a callbox in Strathcorran.

'I've just now seen them off to Inverness,' he told Alison.

'Where? What happened?' She could scarcely hold the phone.

'We went to the doctor's, but he was out on a maternity case and couldn't be reached. His wife gave Jessie an injection of pain-killer, and asked if she should call the ambulance – but you know it has to come miles, and it meant waiting, so Niall decided to take her to hospital himself.'

'And my mother?'

'She's gone too. Listen, Alison, she told me to tell you she'll phone from the hospital as soon as she knows anything. But it could be hours.'

'Yes, I know.' She thought of them driving Jessie the seventy odd miles to Inverness, and caught her breath. Johnny's voice came again. 'And Niall asks if you'll keep André until he returns. His father is away to visit a relative near Torrie.'

'Yes, of course I will. Your Land Rover's here. Will you come back for it?'

'No. If you'll ask Laurie to drive it to Strathcorran for me, and Ian to follow in theirs, it will save me coming back. The keys are in the ignition.' And then he added in a very odd tone: 'In fact, Niall insisted on it. I wonder why?' But Alison was too worried about

Jessie to be puzzled at the meaning of his words. Only later did she remember, and wonder.

After he had hung up she went to tell the Camerons, after first reassuring André about Jessie and his father. Then she made them both a meal, and switched on television for him to watch. She was restless and unable to settle to anything, and found herself watching the phone. It was silly, for working out the distance to Inverness and allowing for traffic and Niall's having to drive carefully, it would be eight before she could expect to hear from her mother, she knew. She looked at the dress material and bundled it away. She tried reading, but even that palled, and in the end she watched the television with André, who had remained glued to the screen, quite fascinated, since it was first switched on.

Then at eight-thirty the phone rang again, and her mother came on after the pips, her voice crackling faintly across the hilly miles between them.

'Alison, I'm sorry, love, I couldn't phone before. I know how you've been waiting for news, but we've just now left Jessie tucked up in a lovely comfortable bed.'

'How is she? What's the matter?'

'They don't know yet. They've taken X-rays of her leg and left arm. They'll know soon enough, and, Alison—'

'Yes?' Alison thought she knew what was coming.

'I've decided to stay here the night. I've just phoned Meg, and she's told me to go over as soon as I finish here. It's the least I can do. Jessie has no one.'

'Of course you must. Shall I put André to bed here?'

'Shall I put Niall on? He's outside the box.'

'No,' Alison said hastily, as the pips went. 'Just tell him André will be safe here. Give Jessie all my love, and try and ring me tomorrow.'

'I will, good-bye—' The phone went dead, and Alison put it down slowly. At least she knew where to reach her mother if she wanted. She told André he could stay the night, and his eyes lit up.

'May I have Rusty on my bed?' he begged.

Alison laughed. 'I'll have to see. And now, I think it's time you went. Come on, I'll give you a good wash, and tell you a nice bedtime story.'

As they went into the bathroom, it began to rain.

The fire was dying down, and Alison was warm and glowing after a hot bath. It was past eleven, and she sat curled up on the settee watching a late film on television, aware of the rain lashing heavily against the windows and drumming on the roof, making the living-room seem so much more warm and secure in comparison. The lamp glowed in the corner, and Rusty lay stretched out on the rug in front of her, her paws twitching as if she dreamed of rabbits. Alison had already moved her basket into her room where André slept soundly, his arms tucked under his head, face a picture of sweet innocence. Alison had stood watching him for a few moments before coming back into the living-room, and she smiled. Niall would come for him in the morning, to take him to the island, and he would enjoy it, and she would have to make sure she was very 'busy', so as not to disillusion a little boy. She turned away, the smile vanishing, and went to make her supper.

The film came to an end, and she stood up yawning, and switched it off, looking at the clock as she did so. It was five minutes to twelve, and there came a knock at the door, a low insistent rat-tat-tat. Rusty jumped up, growling in her throat, and Alison went to the window but could see nothing.

Taking Rusty's collar, she went to the door, heart fast beating, and called: 'Who is it?'

'It's me, Niall MacBain,' was the reply. And she opened the door to see him standing there in the porch, his hair shining wetly from the light behind her. Her heart lurched in a most peculiar way, and she said the first words that came into her head:

'I'm just going to bed.'

'I won't keep you. I've only come to return the blankets,' he answered. 'If you'll hold the door open a moment, I'll fetch them from the car.' His tone was curt, clearly resenting her reluctance, and she flushed and held the door wide, watching him splash wetly across the few yards to his car, then come back carrying the bundle. He wiped his feet on the mat and went into the living-room where he put everything down on a chair. Alison followed him in and said: 'They would have done in the morning.'

'Perhaps, but your mother asked me to call and make sure you were all right,' he answered. His cool grey eyes never left her face. It was disconcerting, and she felt a trace of embarrassment, clad as she was in nightie and dressing-gown. She wanted him to go away. The memory of what had happened the previous day, when he had caught Johnny kissing her, came back strongly. He had looked just like this then – cool and faintly contemptuous. It was none of his business what she did, she thought rebelliously. He had no right to condemn her behaviour, and yet she was tremendously uneasy. To hide the awkward tension that seemed to grow every second, she said: 'I'm fine, thank you, and so is André. I'll have him ready for you in the morning, for you to take to the island.' And then, because of something she didn't understand herself, she added: 'And don't worry, I'll make sure I'm very busy when you come.' And the quick flash of understanding in his eyes was matched by the spark of anger in her own.

Then he smiled. Very slowly, he said: 'Don't tell me you wanted to come too?'

She caught her breath at the sight of that smile, cynical and almost mocking. It stung her to retort: 'With André it would be a pleasure. I've already been with *you*.' And she smiled back.

'And you wouldn't care to repeat it?' he asked softly.

'It was hardly the most enjoyable trip of my life. I love the island, but it's no longer ours.' She took a deep breath. 'I'm very tired.'

'And you'd like me to go?' his mouth quirked. 'As we don't seem able to have a civilized conversation, I think it would be better if I did. After all, I'm not Johnny, am I?' And his long glance, from head to toe, expressed his meaning very clearly.

A warm tide of colour surged into Alison's face. 'And what exactly do you mean by that remark?' she asked, breathing hard, fighting an awful sensation of overwhelming anger.

'You may take it to mean what you like,' he answered coolly. 'If your behaviour in public is any indication—'

'If you're referring to yesterday,' she shot back, 'that was hardly in a *public* place – though I'm quite sure, when the hotel is swarming with your guests, that the gardens will be like Princes Street on a Saturday morning – and if you will sneak around creeping in and out of garages, you must expect to see things occasionally that you're not supposed to.'

One eyebrow lifted fractionally. 'Hardly sneaking. *I* was working.'

Then Alison recalled Johnny's words on the phone, and said: 'I suppose that's why you insisted on the Cameron brothers taking Johnny's Land Rover to Strathcorran – so that he wouldn't come back here?' The tightening of the muscles in his cheek told her she had hit the target, and she went on: 'I must thank you for your keen desire to protect me – but I assure you I don't need protection from *Johnny. He's* a gentleman.'

'And I'm not?' His voice, though still level, had a hard edge to it now, and it gave her a small stab of satisfaction to know that somehow she had managed to flick him on the raw.

'You asked for it,' she glared defiantly up at him. 'Take it how you like.'

'And how does a gentleman kiss, then?' he asked harshly. 'Like this?' And his fingers tightened on her shoulders as he pulled her quickly towards him. His mouth came down on hers, not roughly but strangely gentle. For one absurd moment she tasted the sweetness of his lips, and allowed her body, her treacherous body to relax as she responded, unwilling, yet unable to prevent the surge of strong emotion that swept through her. It hadn't been like that with Johnny. She had felt nothing then. Now – so different – it was so very different. And she realized why and with a faint gasp, managed to wrench herself away. Her mouth trembled uncontrollably as she gasped shakily: 'Get out – *get out*!'

'When I'm ready,' his eyes had gone very dark, frighteningly so. 'I've not finished with you yet.'

'Don't touch me again!' she hissed.

'Frightened?' he taunted. 'Why? I may not be a gentleman, as you made so clear a moment ago, but I don't use force on a woman, ever.'

'You just did,' she retorted, 'when you kissed me.'

'I got the strong impression you enjoyed it. At least, you didn't stop me,' was the soft answer. 'In fact, you were asking for it.'

'You have an odd idea of what constitutes an invitation if you can think that,' she retaliated sharply. 'You didn't buy *me* when you bought the house. Perhaps you'll try and remember that in future.' She moved towards the door of the hall, and held it open. 'And you didn't buy this house either, so I'm perfectly entitled to tell you to leave. Now, will you go?' Then as he turned slowly round, she added: 'You haven't asked to see your son yet. Hadn't you better make sure he's safe?'

His eyes raked her face, and she was startled to see that expression she didn't understand, couldn't fathom. As he went in the hall, she said: 'He's in my bed.'

Alison stood there, trying resolutely not to watch as he walked silently into her bedroom. A moment later he came out. Driven by the desire to hurt him, because he had hurt her and exposed some inner emotions she wanted hidden; and because somehow, this was his Achilles heel, she said breathlessly: 'And after Christmas the school will close, André will have to go to Strathcorran. I won't be teaching him any longer – *that* will make you happy.'

He stopped in his tracks, stopped on his way to the front door, his hair still faintly glistening with rain in the soft light of the hall. And he turned very slowly, and something told Alison that she had gone too far.

'Make me happy?' he repeated, in an odd, harsh tone. 'Why?'

'Don't think I've not noticed the way you are when he's with me. I've seen you. You – you were watching only the other day, when we were on the beach. I saw you. I'm not like you, trying to steal what *you* hold dear. You've taken everything of mine, because that's the way you're made. I'm not like that. I love André because he's a wonderful l-little boy. It's a pity you don't.'

He looked as if she had hit him hard. An icy cold was of something akin to fear filled her. She gasped and moved to go into the living-room and he followed her, closing the door behind him.

'You had better explain that remark,' and his face was white with temper. 'Because I don't intend to leave until you do.'

Alison backed away. He was too close, and too tall. And filled with cold rage. All the pent-up frustration of the past weeks bubbled to the surface, all the resentment she felt about his treatment of his son, and more besides, that she could scarcely understand.

'I'll tell you,' she said. 'You're like a stranger to him. You're so wrapped up in your work you can't see how unhappy he's been – or how pathetically grateful he is because you, at last, have deigned to take him out somewhere with you. Even when you speak of him it's "The boy", or "André", never "My son". Do you think he doesn't feel it? He has a heart, you know, a small one, it's true – but it's full of love. He needs affection – he needs cuddling and h-hugging occasionally, but you can't see—' she broke off, tears perilously near, but she had to go on, had to finish what was in her mind. She took a deep breath. 'And you never speak about your wife. If you have to refer to her, it's always as "André's mother"—'

'Perhaps because she was not my wife.'

The words didn't register for a few moments. Then she realized what he had said. 'You mean you weren't married to her?'

'No.' He stood perfectly still, just watching her.

'Then he—' Alison stopped.

'Then he's illegitimate? Are you frightened to say the word? You surprise me.'

'Oh, I see.'

'I don't think you do at all. In fact, it's time you learned a few basic facts of life, Miss Mackay. One of which is that things aren't always what they seem. And now I'll tell you something else which is absolutely no business of yours, but perhaps you should know. It might give you something to think about.' His words were rapier thrusts of anger, sharp and wounding. 'André is my adopted son. His real father is Duncan, my brother, who had an affair seven years ago with a Brazilian girl in Rio. He was already engaged to someone else, the affair over, when he discovered he was to be a father. He paid money for André's support after that – and never told his wife, who belongs to a wealthy Brazilian ranching family. Then, a few months ago, he heard that André's mother was ill, and asked me to go and see them. He had heard the news too late. She was dead, and André had been sent to an orphanage. The girl's family didn't want anything to do with André; they were too poor, and he was just another mouth to feed, although they had every intention of continuing to take the monthly allowance. It sickened me, this callous indifference to a child, and I made them let me take him from the orphanage. Money still talks, you know. I'm not a sentimental man, but he is my own flesh and blood – and once I'd seen him, I knew—' he stopped and ran his hands over his face. Then he looked at Alison again.

'And you think I neglect André, am like a stranger. That's because, in a way, I am. Or was at first. I'm learning, slowly but surely, to be a real father to him. But you wouldn't understand that – you with your clear-cut instant solutions for everything. I seem to have failed, in your eyes. I'll try and remedy that. And I'm going to take him with me now.'

He turned as if to go to the bedroom. Alison put out her hand.

'Please don't.' It was an effort to speak. 'Please – let him stay. He's deeply asleep. You c-can't disturb him.' Tears were near, but his glance was stonily unmoved. Then he nodded.

'Very well. But I'll be here first thing in the morning.' He walked out, his back broad and straight and unyielding.

Alison crawled to bed in her mother's room, and she couldn't even cry.

CHAPTER NINE

THE next morning Niall came sharp at nine, dressed in sweater and jeans, and carrying a basket of food, and a pair of wellingtons for André.

He nodded formally to Alison as he came in. 'Thank you for having my son. André, say thank you to Miss Mackay for having you.'

He was coldly remote as an unfriendly stranger, completely and utterly different from anything Alison had ever seen. As he and the excited boy went out, he took his son's hand, and André skipped happily along.

Alison stood at the kitchen window and watched them make their way to the boat. Inside her was a leaden grey despair. She had thought she hated Niall MacBain. It had taken a child of six to show her it was really herself she disliked.

Her mother phoned from Meg's to tell her that the X-rays had proved no broken bones, but that Jessie had wrenched a muscle in her leg, and would have to rest it for a while. Then she hesitated, and Alison sensed reluctance to say something else. Gently she asked: 'What is it?'

'Well, Jessie can come home on Tuesday. I was wondering if you'd mind me staying on at Meg's until then?'

'Why, of course.' She had a sharp pang of inner dismay. Was her mother so nervous of her reaction that she had dreaded telling her? More quietly, she added: 'You've been working so hard. A few days away from home will do you good – and I'll manage fine.'

'You will, dear? That's a load off my mind. You'll explain to Niall?'

'Of course. And I'll phone you this evening. Give Jessie all my love, and will you take her some flowers from me?'

They spoke for a few minutes more, and then Alison chatted to Meg before hanging up thoughtfully.

She was having her eyes opened about herself, and she wasn't sure if she liked the experience. It was rather sobering to realize how selfishly she had been behaving. She had fought against her mother selling the house – most of all against the man who was even now transforming it; Niall MacBain, who had adopted his brother's son because nobody wanted him. It was a big step for anyone to take, but he hadn't hesitated. And Alison had accused him of not caring. Truly she had a lot to learn, and her first lesson had taken place the previous night. The first – and undoubtedly the last, for something told Alison there would be no more talking with Niall MacBain. She could not erase from her mind the expression he had worn when he had finished telling her about André. There was a certain pride, a look almost of nobility.

Niall was a true man, a gentle man in the best sense of the word, and all her scorn had been as nothing against his strength of purpose, and his sense of honour.

She walking into the living-room, and looked around her. Her face was drawn and tired, for she had slept little after Niall had gone. There was a yawning emptiness about the house that had nothing to do with her mother or Jessie being away.

The room was untidy. Jessie would have to rest, and would be unable to do housework. And Alison, with the days stretching blankly ahead, had to do something to fill the vacuum. She collected all the cleaning materials and polishes, dressed in her oldest clothes, and began to clean the house.

At six o'clock she sat down for a welcome cup of tea in the kitchen, tired both physically and mentally. She had worked so hard that she managed to keep from thinking, but now as she tried to relax, the thoughts came rushing back.

Alison drank the tea and pushed the cup away restlessly. If only she could go somewhere away from here, to sort everything out in her mind. If only . . . then she saw the boat bobbing gently on its mooring. They had returned, and gone home without a word. She stood up impatiently. What had she expected? Niall to come and tell her how the picnic had gone? She smiled bitterly and went to the window. The boat was inviting, swayed gently by small wavelets, the outboard motor still attached. Why not? She looked at it again, then at Rusty. A boat ride to the island would clear her head she knew, perhaps help her to sleep when the night came, and she was utterly alone.

'You want to come?' Alison asked the dog, and Rusty wagged her tail and stretched. They went out, and as they passed the line of washing billowing in the breeze, she felt it. It was nearly dry. When they came back it would be ready to take in and iron – something else to help pass the long evening.

The sky was bright, the clouds hurrying past high

and fast, and the gulls crying harshly as they wheeled overhead. They would be watching her, beady eyes bright on the boat as she started the motor, pulling the string to whirr it to life. Some would follow them to the island, anticipating fish for supper. But Alison wasn't away fishing. There was something she had to think about and she would do it better on the island, might remember what it was that pressed at the back of her mind as irritating as a speck of sand in an oyster, and growing just as surely. Rusty crouched down as they set off swiftly. Not for her the stiff breeze. She preferred to lie as flat as possible until they reached their destination. Rusty loved the island, for it had new smells to sniff out in the undergrowth, and the infinitely long journey, as it must have seemed to her, was well worth it.

Alison looked back, saw distantly Niall's car, several children playing on the shore, and a dog barking furiously at the gulls, the noise carrying clearly over the surface of the water, even above the put-put of the motor as they sped along. She sighed and turned to look ahead. The island loomed closer and darker as they neared it. She wondered what had been in André's mind as he went to it for the first time that morning. Excitement, naturally, perhaps tinged with fear, for it did look rather grim and forbidding from this side. But with Niall he would know that he would be safe. And he would scamper out on to the shingle and run about excitedly, waiting for the picnic to begin.

So vivid were the pictures conjured up that Alison blinked hard. She hoped that he had enjoyed it. She wanted so very much for him to be happy, and perhaps he would be now, after such an unfortunate start to his life. For whatever Alison had said and thought about Niall MacBain, one thing she knew deep down, and that was that his words, spoken so bitterly and forcefully to her the previous night, had been true. He was learning to be a father to André, a real father. He would be a good one, just and fair, and never cruel, for even as a boy he had had a strong sense of justice, and . . .

Alison drew in breath sharply as the boat bumped against the beach. She knew now what had been nagging at the back of her mind for days, knew in a blinding flash of revelation exactly what she had been fighting all these weeks. The knowledge flooded her mind, pushing everything else out, and she jumped from the boat after Rusty, skidding on the slippery shingle as she landed. She caught her balance, then walked quickly along the beach, away from Shielbaig, round to the other side of the island.

She knew it, yet still she would not put it into words. Knew why, now, she had fought so hard to prevent Niall from coming into her life, knew why she had always had the breathless heart-stopping sensation whenever he was near. The prickly antagonism had been a defence – and a poor one – against her woman's heart, the foolish heart that had finally betrayed her. And now she could say the words. As she went the last few steps to reach the warmer, Skye-facing side of the island, she said them out loud: 'I love Niall MacBain.'

Rusty looked up from her eternal sniffing and wagged her tail as if in agreement. Tears filled Alison's eyes. She loved a man, had done, she knew now, for years, and he despised her, thought of her as selfish and spoilt. How he would laugh if he knew! How ironic that he should in the end, take her heart, after she had fought so bitterly against him. She went and sat on a flat rock, still shaken after her belated discovery. All the little things she had tried to ignore came strongly to the fore as she gazed out over the sea, and she remembered the one thing that she had deliberately forgotten for so many – too many years.

It had happened at school, when she was nearly six and Alec and Niall had been eleven. Miss Carmichael, their stern but much loved schoolmistress, had gone out to talk to the mailman, leaving the children working. An inky pellet had landed on Alec's desk, and he had immediately gone over to Niall and accused him of spoiling his exercise book.

Next second, inevitably, a fight had started, and Alison, fearful that Miss Carmichael would hear and return, had rushed impulsively to stop it. Too impulsively, for a flying fist had caught her ribs and sent her staggering back. As she cried out, they had stopped and, seeing her white face, had come shamefacedly to their feet.

Then a strange thing had happened. Niall, the sworn enemy, had come to where she stood crying holding her side, and said, completely ignoring the astonished stares of Alec and the other children who surrounded them: 'If it was me that hit you, Alison, I'm sorry, it was an accident.' And there had been only concern on his face, nothing else. But she had remembered it because of that, and the look in his eyes had remained locked away in some secret memory chest every since. Perhaps because even at nearly six, she had recognized true gallantry when she saw it.

She bent restlessly and picked up a few pebbles, and began to flick them into the water, as she watched the black waves rush up the sand and recede with a slight shushing sound. A gull swooped down to the surface, then rose again, soaring effortlessly upwards with sad harsh cries as if disappointed at seeing no fish.

It was no use. The closure of the school would give her an opportunity she must take; to get away from Shielbaig. She would apply for a transfer immediately, perhaps to Inverness or Edinburgh, and there she would try and forget what had happened, and maybe she would forget Niall in time. For she would not be able to bear the bitter-sweet agony of seeing him every day, of living within a few hundred yards of him and André, and torturing herself, wondering what he was doing, where he was going, and why ... she would come home at week-ends, but with care she wouldn't have to see him. She would tell her mother, and Jessie. Jessie, with her shrewd mind, probably wouldn't be surprised at all. Several things she had said recently now seemed, in the light of Alison's new-found knowledge, to have been remarkably astute. Perhaps she guessed Alison's feelings, and had wondered ...

Alison looked up as she felt a heavy drop of rain on her hand. The sky had grown darker, and some of the warmth had gone. She looked towards the Cuillins, but they had vanished in a grey mist.

'Come on, Rusty!' she called, and the dog galloped up. They set off back. It had been a mistake to come, she knew, for the bitter realization of her feelings had brought only sadness with it. She walked round the bend, and saw the beach, and it was empty. Alison stared in disbelief, wondering if she had made a mistake . . . Then she saw the boat bobbing all alone in the water. In her haste to land, and with the chaotic thoughts jostling, she had forgotten to secure it. She had no way of getting home. Even as Alison stood there watching helplessly, it drifted even further away, and the heavens opened and the rain lashed down.

CHAPTER TEN

ALISON stood in the shelter of the trees, wondering if she could swim that far. But even as she debated, knowing the dangers, she realized with sinking heart that it was no use. The current was too strong. She would be exhausted before she was half-way, and if Rusty decided to follow her ... Already the leaves were heavy with rain, and began to tip over, huge drops coursing accurately down on her. She looked up at the steep slope behind her.

'Rusty, come on, girl,' she commanded, and began to scramble up the rocky incline towards the cottage. There was no thought in her mind other than the immediate problem of shelter. She dared not think ahead yet.

It was only as Alison stood in the open doorway looking out at a dripping wet world of green and grey that she realized the full gravity of the situation. There was no one at home to miss them. It was Saturday night, and going rapidly darker with swollen rain clouds overhead. She shuddered, helpless in the face of an overwhelming sense of utter loneliness, and thought of her mother who would phone, and phone again, and wonder ... She had no matches to light a fire, and no food. Alison swallowed hard, and looked around her. It was no time for tears or self-pity, and she couldn't stand up all night, so she might as well try and see what advantages were to be gained from her shelter, before the light grew too poor to look by.

The cottage had a stone floor, littered with dead leaves and twigs. There were four rooms altogether, two up and two down, connected by a crude wooden staircase. She looked through, and there was nothing anywhere to sit down on, and as she finished, she went to the stairs, sat on the bottom one, and drew Rusty to her.

'Well, old girl, you'll go hungry tonight,' she whispered. 'And I'm sorry. But I'm glad I've brought you with me.' Rusty's soft brown eyes gazed up into Alison's, and she bent impulsively and hugged her. The dog's coat was still damp from the rain, and she whined softly as Alison held her.

She would remember this day for the rest of her life, she knew. Not only for the awful sense of being marooned, but because she had discovered the overwhelming fact that she was in love, painfully in love, for the first time in her life.

They sat there quietly, listening to the rain because there was nothing else to do. The image of Niall's face was everywhere. Alison dared not close her eyes because she knew she would see him as he had been the previous night, lashing her with his contempt. She moved awkwardly as the hard stairs pressed into her back. No, she wouldn't forget this.

She wasn't afraid of the dark, or being alone, yet there was an indefinable sense of eeriness about the place, some atmosphere dredged from the mists of the past. It was nonsense, of course, but it was almost as if she were not alone, as if others, long-dead Mackays – and others – waited with her.

She must eventually have slept, and had an odd dream, in which she heard someone call her name, and call it again, and so vivid was it that she awoke and sat up to find Rusty gone. Heart hammering against her ribs, she stood up a little shakily and found her shoes which she'd kicked off, then went to the door.

'Rusty, Rusty!' she called, and heard a faint answering bark, then a voice shouting: 'Alison!'

She hadn't been dreaming, it was real! She ran out of the cottage, into pitch blackness, the rain lashing down heavier than ever as she sped along the path, heedless of the danger in the dark. The rain mingled with the tears that coursed down her face, tears of joy that blinded her so that she ran straight into the blurred figure that suddenly loomed up from the darkness. Then she was held tightly in a pair of powerful arms as she heard a most familiar voice say: 'Thank God! Thank God! I thought you were dead!'

She opened her eyes, and it was Niall who held her. She gasped painfully, whispered: 'Oh, no, it's you!' and tried to pull herself away.

'Don't – don't fight. Let me hold you.' Strangely, his voice trembled. Alison gazed up at him, saw his hair and face running with water as he looked down at her, and she took a deep breath. And then she knew.

They looked at each other, there in that bleak coldness of pouring rain, and he lifted his hand gently to touch her face.

In a voice that shook, he said: 'I thought you were dead.'

'I was here – in the cottage – the boat—' she began.

'Yes, I know now. I saw it drifting – then I saw your washing, all hung out in the pouring rain, and I knew that something was terribly wrong.' His arms tightened around her. 'I had to make sure, so I went to the cottage – and it was cold and empty, and your cup was on the table, and Rusty was gone – and I knew.' He suddenly bent his head, burying it in her hair. 'Oh, my God, that was when the nightmare began. I took a boat, I don't know whose, and set out, and I was hoping you'd be in the other, but when I saw it empty—' he stopped.

They were so drenched with rain that their clothes were as shiny sealskin, but Alison couldn't have moved away for anything on earth, nor did she want to. A growing wonder filled her heart, swelling every moment as she heard his words. She hastened to tell him, 'I'm sorry, it was all my fault. I'd come here to think, and I'd not secured it – and—'

'No, it doesn't matter. Don't you see, Alison? It doesn't matter. All that counts is that you're safe.' Trembling, like a man possessed, his mouth found hers and for endless seconds they clung together, filled with a kind of precious wonder. The rain was sweet on his lips, sweet and cool, and the kiss was warm, and of such infinite tenderness that she could scarcely breathe or think, only know the ecstasy of his mouth on hers.

Then shakily he said: 'We must go. You're soaked to the skin. We must go home now.'

'Yes.' Her teeth were chattering with the cold, and with reaction. She could not believe that it was happening. It was not possible. Yet the rain and the cold were painfully real. They made their slippery way down to where the two boats were secured together, and Rusty woofed apologetically, as if for leaving her.

'We'll go in ours, it's a better engine,' Niall said, as he helped Alison in, and it seemed odd to her that he said 'ours'. It was his boat now. Rusty sat beside her in the bows, Niall started the motor, and they set off through the icy driving rain, now intensified in force with their speed. The island receded, barely visible, and they were alone in a vast grey wilderness of water. Niall stood in the stern, guiding them, his eyes on Alison's face, never looking away. She looked back at him, and something sparked between them. Almost electric, like fire, their glances met and held. There was no need for words.

She was shivering violently when they beached the boat outside Courthill. Niall swung her up into his arms and carried her home. In the kitchen he put her down.

'Go and get yourself dry,' he ordered. 'I'm going to Courthill for my working clothes.'

'Yes – yes, I will.' She went to do his bidding. When she padded into the kitchen after changing into warm sweater and trews, he was crouching down, wearing his old jeans and paint-spattered sweater, and briskly rubbing Rusty with an old towel.

He looked up, saw Alison, and gave Rusty a smack. 'That's enough for you, old girl.' Then he stood and came towards her, and Alison waited. Slowly he lifted his hands and took hers in his. The clasp was warm and firm, and her heart beat so fast that she could scarcely breathe.

'Alison,' he said.

'Yes, Niall?'

'You know, don't you?' His voice was low and

gentle, and she couldn't take her eyes from his face, his dear sweet face, the one she saw in so many dreams.

'Yes, I know,' she answered, and his face became blurred. Then suddenly, wordlessly, they were clinging together in the warm haven of the kitchen, and their mouths told them what words could not.

And later, after they had eaten toast and hot soup, an ordinary enough meal, yet with him a banquet, they sat on the settee in front of a roaring fire in the living-room. Rusty lay sprawled out on the rug at their feet, well fed, fast asleep, content. Niall's arm was tightly round Alison, as if he would never let her go, and that was right.

'When did you know?' he asked.

'This afternoon. I went to the island to try and think, because after last night I knew – I thought I knew that you despised me, and I had to get away. I was planning how I would get a transfer and work in Inverness – or Edinburgh – anywhere to get away from you.'

He groaned and turned towards her, his face softer and gentler in the glow of the fire. 'And I would have let you go. My stiff-necked pride would have let me watch you go away – oh, Alison, I've been a brute and a swine, I—'

'No,' she put a finger to his lips. 'No, you haven't, it was me – I hated you because you were taking everything from me – but I didn't realize, all the time, that I was fighting this growing attraction to you, this awareness of everything you were, and did. It wasn't until I reached the island this afternoon that I finally knew I loved you.' She paused. 'I was so stunned by the realization that I forgot to secure the boat.'

He began to laugh softly, his fingers playing lightly

184

up and down her arm. 'And it wasn't until I saw the boat that I realized you were the whole world to me—' He suddenly sobered, and went on more quietly: 'All the time, these past years, you've been in my mind, just there, quietly at the back of my thoughts. And always I remembered our last meeting, in the woods.'

He must have felt her stir uneasily, for he drew a deep breath. 'And you hadn't forgotten it either, had you?'

'No, how could I? Perhaps that was where it began, there by the trout stream that night.'

'Yes, I think it did. You were so beautiful, Alison, so proud and defiant as you told me to go. I wanted so desperately to kiss you.' He seemed faintly surprised, as if the memories were rushing back faster than he knew. 'Somehow, the thought of you was always bound up in the house, as if you belonged together. I always loved Courthill, always envied you and Alec for being able to live in it, especially when—' he stopped.

'Go on, please,' she prompted.

'Och well, you know that time you asked me why I'd said it should really be mine?'

Her heartbeats quickened. 'If you don't want to tell me, it's all right—'

'No, I can tell you now, Alison. There are no more secrets between us any more.' Their eyes met and held, and Niall's were so full of love that she almost cried out.

'I learned when I was a boy that there was more, that had been kept well hidden. There had been smuggling, and whisky-making – on the island, I believe – over a hundred years ago. Our families were tied up in more ways than one. Two of our great-great-grandparents were inveterate gamblers, only yours wasn't so lucky, and when he was on a bad streak one night, he staked Courthill and lost. But before the deeds could be transferred to the MacBains, someone gave the game away about the whisky and the smuggling to the Customs man – and my ancestor went to prison. Yours didn't. Nobody ever found out how it had happened, but you can imagine the rumours flying around, then when the two boys fell for the same girl – everything erupted. The feud was well and truly on.'

His story shook Alison. She raised anguished eyes to him.

'Then all this time—'

'No,' his lips silenced her worried question. 'What's past is done. How can we *know* the truth after all this time? But it's something I believed when I was a boy, and you know how a child's mind works. It helped to feed the fires when I wanted a scrap.'

'I know,' she smiled. 'You were always fighting, both of you. Perhaps, without the feud, you might have been good friends?'

He grinned. 'Perhaps. But life wouldn't have been half so much fun. I'll never forget those days – nor you. Oh, Alison, I've been so jealous every time I've seen you with Johnny – I just wanted to hurt you.'

'And I you. And all the time, as I grew more fond of André, I thought how I mustn't because he was yours, and – oh, Niall, I was jealous too, in a very different way.'

'He loves you. Alison. He's always talking about you, asking if you'll look after him when he's older.'

She drew breath sharply. 'And I was going to—'

'No, don't say it. I need you, Alison, very much. I've

never wanted anyone as much as I want you. Everything about you – you drove me mad at times, until I couldn't stand it any more, which is when I did the only thing possible – kissed you!' He laughed, and held her tighter, joyously. 'But I didn't realize the effect it would have on me!'

'Oh, Niall, don't worry. I'll work at Strathcorran school as long as I can, and look after—'

'I don't mean teaching. I mean as my wife, with André and me, at Courthill, to be together for always.'

'Oh, Niall darling, I love you so much. Yes, oh, yes!'

And his kiss was more wonderful than anything else in the world.

Mills & Boon Classics

The very best of Mills & Boon
romances, brought back for those of you
who missed reading them when they
were first published.

There are three other Classics for you to collect this
August

SILVER FRUIT UPON SILVER TREES
by Anne Mather

It would be easy, Eve told Sophie. All she had to do was to go
to Trinidad and pretend to be the granddaughter of the wealthy
Brandt St Vincente for four weeks and the money she needed
would be hers. But when Sophie met the disturbing Edge St
Vincente, who thought she was his niece, and fell in love with
him, she realised that perhaps it wasn't going to be that simple
after all . . .

THE REAL THING
by Lilian Peake

The job Cleone Aston had just been offered — editor of a
fashion magazine — was going to be tremendously thrilling, and
demanding, after her job as reporter on a local newspaper. But
the biggest challenge was to come from her new boss — Ellis
Firse.

COUSIN MARK
by Elizabeth Ashton

Damaris loved her home, Ravenscrag, more than anything else
in the world — and the only way she could keep it under the
terms of her grandfather's will, was to marry his heir, her
unknown cousin Mark. So she must be very careful not to fall
in love elsewhere, Damaris told herself firmly when she met
the attractive Christian Trevor.

If you have difficulty in obtaining any of these books through
your local paperback retailer, write to:

Mills & Boon Reader Service
P.O. Box 236, Thornton Road, Croydon, Surrey, CR9 3RU.

Mills & Boon Classics

The very best of Mills & Boon
romances, brought back for those of you
who missed reading them when they
were first published.

In
September
we bring back the following four
great romantic titles.

NO FRIEND OF MINE
by Lilian Peake

Lester Kings was her brother's friend, not hers, Elise told herself
firmly. She had never liked him when she was a child, and now
he had come back into their lives the old antagonism was there
still, as strong as ever. Yet somehow she just couldn't stop
thinking about him . . .

SHADE OF THE PALMS
by Roberta Leigh

To Stephen Brandon, Julia was no more than Miss Watson, his
unflappable, highly efficient secretary. A dowdy woman wearing
unfashionable clothes, sensible shoes and spectacles, he would
have thought if he'd considered the matter at all. But he was to
discover that appearances can be deceptive and that there was a
totally unexpected side to Julia . . .

THE BRIDE OF ROMANO
by Rebecca Stratton

It was the charming Paolo Veronese who had got Storm the job
of governess to the little Gino in southern Italy, but it was
Gino's stern guardian, Alexei Romano, who caused her all the
heart-searching. She knew that in getting involved with Alexei
she would be utterly outclassed, but all the same . . .

THE ARROGANCE OF LOVE
by Anne Mather

Dominic Halstad was the most attractive man Susan had ever
met, and made her rather difficult fiancé David seem dull by
comparison. But even if her first loyalty were not to David, what
right had she to think about Dominic — a married man?

Doctor Nurse Romances

and August's
stories of romantic relationships behind the scenes
of modern medical life are:

PRIZE OF GOLD
by Hazel Fisher

It was the eminent surgeon, Sir Carlton Hunter, who
told Sandie that love was the prize of gold — but she
was determined to win the gold medal for the best
student nurse, rather than lose her heart!
Unfortunately, it was also Sir Carlton who was wreck-
ing her chances of winning either prize . . . .

DOCTOR ON BOARD
(The Path of the Moonfish)
by Betty Beaty

To meet Paul Vansini at the very beginning of her first
cruise as a hostess aboard the luxury liner *Pallas Athene*,
should have made Cristie Cummings perfectly happy.
And so it might have done, but for Doctor David
Lindsay's cutting remarks!